Reap the Harvest

J. Burke Hatfield

PublishAmerica
Baltimore

© 2002 by J. Burke Hatfield.

All rights reserved. No part of this book may be reproduced in any form without written permission from the publishers, except by a reviewer who may quote brief passages in a review to be printed in a newspaper or magazine.

First printing

To: Irene Overkat
Hope you enjoy!
J Burke Hatfield

ISBN: 1-59129-376-6
PUBLISHED BY PUBLISHAMERICA BOOK PUBLISHERS
www.publishamerica.com
Baltimore

Printed in the United States of America

This book is dedicated to my mother, who gave her life in giving me mine, and to my father, who taught me to see things as they are, not as you want them to be. To my wife, Celesta, my son, Mark and my daughter, Gerri, who lifted me up and made me go forward when my determination waned.

Acknowledgments:

A special thank you to Naomi Mathews; without her dedication and long hours of typing, including numerous changes and rewrites, this book would not have come to fruition. I also wish to thank Sally Jo Kane for her valued review of the text and appropriate comments, and Gail O'Brien for her efforts in helping me meet the requirements of the publishers for submission of the final text and supporting documentation. Finally, to the staff of PublishAmerica who believed in the story and brought my dream to reality.

Chapter 1

George Sternvald awoke refreshed from a deep sleep. Although but fifteen, his body was lean and hard, shoulders exceptionally broad for one his age. His dark straight hair, cropped short for comfort during the humid summer days, topped a face showing the initial lines of manhood. Deep-set grey-blue eyes twinkled with mirth whenever a smile lit his countenance.

Very soon the family would reach his father's goal of freedom, America. He was proud that he had studied and learned the English language while in school. He felt confident he could help his father, Otto, in the upcoming days. George had spent considerable time reading and rereading the pamphlets about America and specifically Aurora, Washington. Many hours were spent with Papa, huddled together, planning an orchard, a home and outbuildings on land they were yet to see.

The selling of the family farm in Weserburg, Germany and the time-consuming barge trip to Bremerhaven to board the Norwegian vessel, *Kongsberg*, to America seemed to capsulize into a few days in George's mind. He hoped the anger of his mother, Gretchen, toward Otto and him would fade, but he feared the opposite might be true predicated on his mother's indifferent attitude during the ocean voyage.

George's thoughts turned back to the days just before leaving the farm in Weserburg:

"Tired?"

"No, just daydreaming a little," George answered, as his father sat down beside him on the farmhouse back porch.

"Daydreaming is good, as long as one doesn't daydream too

much."

"I'm not sure I understand," George said.

"Making daydreams is easy; making your daydreams come true, that's the tough part. Expect to be disappointed at times."

"Is that why we are leaving? Your disappointments?"

"In part, but it's really to follow my dream of going to America."

"I think I understand."

"Understand this too: do not respect or trust a man with money; 'The love of money is the root of all evil' and that love can rob one of self-respect and dignity. It often came by ill-gotten means."

"Money can do good or evil, I would think."

"You have much to learn. I want you to pledge to me that you will always keep the family together. Also know that a man is of no value if he gains everything material but loses his family. Keep the fabric tightly woven; wear it as a shield around you and those you love. There is no greater joy, no sacrifice too much. One more thought: think of your life as a season. In the spring, when you are young and vigorous, you plant. In summer, you cultivate, weed, water, and take pride in your efforts. Storms might come, some plants are lost, but you go on tending, sweating—yes, praying a little. Fall, when you are older, wiser to see, understand and appreciate the fruits of your labor—you will reap the harvest of your hard work. Winter brings death. The vigorous plants become old, brittle, battle-scarred from the long season. Your harvest is over and how well you planted, how well you tended, how much you loved is reflected in you and the seeds you will plant the following spring. We are fortunate as farmers to have seasons follow seasons. In life, we have but one season and we are judged by the harvest we have reaped."

One evening while Otto and the children stayed on deck, Gretchen had done some much-needed laundry, then returned to the stateroom. Hot and tired, she slipped from her damp clothes and undergarments, then stepped into the shower. The sharp sting of spray invigorated her face and body. With her eyes closed and tight muscles now relaxing, she stood for a long moment before slowly soaping her face and body, washing her long, coal-black hair until it squeaked between her fingers. She could feel the strain and worry of the journey draining away. Except for an occasional tug at her heart when she thought of the Weserburg farm, she had few regrets. She quickly toweled herself, wrapping a dry towel around the still-damp hair now piled on top her head. The air in the cabin was cool by comparison to the confines of the tiny bathroom. Hurriedly she slipped into her favorite flannel housecoat and sat on the edge of her bed, working the damp strands of hair against the towel. Hair now dry, she moved to the mirror where she brushed her hair to a high sheen, its slight natural curl framing her oval face. A soft smile touched the corners of her mouth. She examined her face clinically: high, smooth forehead; black even-lined brows; bright, deep-set dark eyes; a straight nose; full, soft lips covering clean, even teeth; a strong chin. She felt her body sending messages of desire for Otto's touch.

Chapter 2

The loud, complaining cry of sea gulls edged into George Sternvald's sleep. *Sea gulls?* He'd not heard that sound since two days out on the English Channel. They must be getting close to America. George thought back, trying to bring into mental focus the large chart-map shown to him by Jan, a young Norwegian sailor he had befriended earlier in the week. No mid-Atlantic islands on the route that he could recall. It must be America. He quietly slipped from beneath the blankets and padded, barefoot, to the small stateroom porthole. He could see nothing but blue-green ocean capped occasionally by a curling whitecap. Two gulls swept by the opening, ducking and darting, then gliding up and away on the air currents.

He dressed quietly, not wishing to disturb Anna, his nine-year-old sister sleeping peacefully in her bunk, and stepped into the corridor. The morning sun had burst from its hiding place beyond the northeast horizon, dispelling a thin fog bank that partially obscured the seascape.

Walking to the port railing, he leaned against it and looked down at the churning water rushing alongside the ship. Overhead and to the stern he spotted more gulls, wings spread wide, drifting in the freighter's air slip.

Gradually the deck filled with passengers, as they too took in the morning air. An undercurrent of anticipation ran through the crowd as most realized the significance of the gulls' presence.

Jan strolled by on his way to the bridge, occasionally stopping to pass the time with passengers.

"Good morning, George," Jan called out cheerily.

"I see we have guests this morning," George said.

"Oh, yes, they come to meet us, weather permitting, every trip."

"We should be in New York today, then!"

"By afternoon, perhaps."

George walked the deck, nodding to passengers whom he had met over the last two weeks and had become nodding acquaintances.

A few minutes later Otto joined George on deck. "I have some papers to go over with you." Otto steered George to a quiet area just off the main deck and pulled a much-folded envelope from his hip pocket. "Our letter of credit to the bank. It is in both our names. If we need money, go to a bank, show them this letter and proof of who you are, and draw out funds. You need to sign." Otto retrieved a pen and ink well from a writing desk and George signed the document "You know about the extra money? Where I keep it?"

"Yes, Papa. Don't worry."

Chapter 3

Shipping activity in and out of New York had slowed dramatically. A stubborn morning mist lingered, held captive by a warm upper inversion. As the freighter moved slowly past the Coney Island Lighthouse and into the narrow ship channel leading to Upper New York Bay, the din of the harbor grew louder. Foghorns and whistles bellowed for attention; vessels cautiously jockeyed for position. A light wind opened small windows in the fog, allowing the passengers a glimpse of Brooklyn and Staten Island. Then silently the fog closed ranks. Dimly silhouetted against a backdrop of darkened sky, tall buildings stood as sentinels and silently observed activities in the major world seaport.

By three o'clock the mist and fog had, if anything, thickened. The *Kongsberg* eased to a stop, the engines whispering as they held the ship motionless. Jan and Jared, a fellow sailor, hurried by with two companions, heading for the bow. Soon the clanking of the twin anchors could be heard as they were lowered into the dark, blue grey water. The ship lurched, then stilled as the anchors set into the bay's silty bottom several fathoms below. The engines ceased for the first time since departure, some sixteen days before. The sudden silence shattered only by the melancholy, throaty blasts from the *Kongsberg's* foghorn as it joined with others in an anthem to the fog.

The chorus sang on and on, until early next morning when a sudden wind moved down the Hudson River, sweeping the channels clean, freshening the morning with a crisp, invigorating sting. The bay and city stood sparkling and fresh at early dawn. Ahead and to port stood the Statue of Liberty, arm held high, the torch bright and aflame with the first rays of the sun rising over the ocean, heralding in a beautiful September morning.

At that moment Anna and George, unable to sleep, chose to come on deck. "Oh, there she is," whispered Anna. "My lady!" She grasped George's hand, her nails digging into his palm. He squeezed back, gently. Tears welled in Anna's eyes. The copper outer body, not tarnished as it would in years to come, reflected back the sun, casting a shimmering glow, the beacon-torch dimming as the full light of day hit her graceful form. Morning sunlight winked from the many-paned windows lining the waterfront and the taller buildings behind. To the left the low Appalachian foothills of New Jersey stood stark brown and green against a chill blue sky. Here and there an occasional groves of oak, festooned in mantles of golden yellows and burnt red leaves, dotted the landscape.

Although it was early, the wharves teemed with activity. Fishing boats capable of plying the ocean puffed out to sea, their nets hung from rigging appearing as tattered sails. Tugs with barges in tow moved slowly, the rhythmic beat of their powerful engines echoing back from shore. Ferryboats, low in the water, moved swiftly along appointed routes, carrying passengers across the busy harbor. Here and there anchored freighters exhausted smoke and steam from their stacks; others sat unmoved, some high in the water awaiting cargo, others loaded to the painted water line, impatient to empty the holds.

The *Kongsberg* shuddered to life. The low, throaty engine's noise reverberating throughout the ship awakened Otto and Gretchen. Looking out the porthole, Otto could see the clear morning.

"The fog has lifted, it's a beautiful day. Let's dress and go see Anna's lady!"

"I'm tired, Otto. Let me stay in bed," Gretchen pleaded sleepily. She rolled to her side, feigning sleep.

He hurried into his clothes and went to find Anna and George, who stood among a cluster of passengers surveying the panorama before them. "What a grand day!" Otto said, as he pushed through to take a place beside the two youngsters at the railing. Fascinated by all about him, Otto drank in the scene, scarcely believing its enormity.

Jared and Jan had broken from the group earlier, and with the rest of the crew were making preparation for docking at Ellis Island. The anchors were pulled into the bow stations, hosed of accumulated silt and seaweed. Dark smoke belched from the exhaust funnel. An air of expectation gripped those aboard.

Chapter 4

In her room, Gretchen sighed and slumped down on the edge of the unmade bed. Her thoughts drifted back over the last weeks. A torrent of regrets washed over her. Why had she allowed herself to be convinced of this folly? On the other hand, the trip and change of scene had been a pleasant respite from the sameness and drudgery of farm life. Still, was she not exchanging that life of certainty for one of uncertainty and perhaps untold hardships? She envied George his ability to speak the new language of America and the optimistic attitude that comes so often with youth.

Otto, too, was excited. His strength and determination had bolstered her, forcing her to think in a positive way, dispelling fears, at least for the time being. Remembering back to Otto's impact on the farm, his strength of will and support during her father's illness and after, she was suddenly swept with overwhelming thanksgiving. He was such a loving man, so gentle, concerned, thoughtful, and understanding of the moodiness that overtook her at times.

Feeling better now, spirits lifted, she set about final packing, humming a tune she had not recalled since her childhood, then went to find her family topside.

The docking procedure at Ellis Island took an hour, as the freighter was pushed to a vacant slip next to others. A large passenger liner of unknown vintage and in a state of serious disrepair towered above the *Kongsberg*. Hundreds of people, young and old, dressed in a myriad of styles, designs, colors, and condition crowded the two decks or hung from portholes, waving and yelling in a babble of incoherent noise. Men in uniform ran about the decks, pushing and coaxing, their shouts adding to the confusion, while they tried in vain to bring order.

"Thank God we're not with them," Gretchen said appreciatively. "What an awful way to live!" Anna and George watched in amazement as the human anthill seemed to swarm about aimlessly.

Jan and his companion Jared were heavensent. Well-trained and alert to passenger needs, they quietly gathered the passengers together and explained the basic procedures to expect inside the large processing center on Ellis Island. They patiently answered questions, then helped with the unloading of passengers and hand luggage.

Household goods and large trunks, such as that of the Sternvalds, would be unloaded and housed in a terminal on the New Jersey side. Passengers would be ferried from Ellis to the New Jersey docks, or those wishing to go to New York could catch other ferries crossing the Hudson to docks situated near Battery Park on Manhattan Island.

Otto and George sought out Jan, thanking him for all his help and kindness during the trip. Otto pressed some coins into his hand as they said good-bye.

Fortunately, the *Kongsberg* passengers gained access to the processing center well ahead of the horde on the rusting passenger ship. Even so, the hall was crowded and warm. The smell of unwashed bodies and clothing permeated the air.

Government clerks sat behind a row of long tables placed against the far wall. Groups of emigrants milled about, mostly in family clusters, waiting patiently for the line to move forward. A balcony housed the administrative offices and a handful of small cubicles where doctors examined suspected cases of lung, skin, or eye disorders. If rejected, the patient was tagged and sent back to the country of origin, with or without his or her family, depending on the family status or monetary circumstances. Despite the backup caused by yesterday's weather and the large crowd, the lines moved briskly, the clerks taking a minimum of time to clear each applicant.

"I will handle this. It is the father's place to conduct business."

"All right, Papa," George said with reservation.

"Name?" the clerk asked flatly, not looking up. He spoke in English.

Otto looked puzzled.

"Your name, Papa," prompted George.

"Oh! Otto, my name is Otto," he said in German. "Otto Sternvald."

"Just your surname, please." Otto again looked bewildered.

"Give him our last name first and your first name last," George again prompted his father.

"*Ja*," Otto said, understanding now. Slowly, he said, "Sternvald, Otto."

"Finally," said the clerk as he filled in the form. "Country of origin?"

Again Otto was confused. "George, you handle this," Otto said.

"You speak English?" the clerk asked hopefully.

"Yes, sir."

"Good. What country do you come from?"

"Germany."

"Destination? Uh, where do you go from here?"

"Aurora... Aurora, Washington."

"Any illness? Black lung, eye problems, history of cholera?"

"No, none."

"Thank you." The clerk's attitude was less surly. He glanced up. "This is your family?"

"Yes, sir." The clerk pulled three more forms from his stack and scrawled the last name on each, then quickly obtained the names and ages of the family, signed and stamped each form and handed them up to George. "Here you are. Welcome to America. Next!"

They walked through a narrow passageway, single file, as a man in a white jacket, perhaps a young doctor or nurse, briefly examined each one's eyes, teeth, general color. Satisfied, he affixed an ink seal on each form and motioned them on. Happily, the Sternvalds moved under the overhanging balcony and to a large door leading to the outside. On each side of the doorway stood a burly guard, handgun strapped in a belt holster, billy club hanging loosely from its snap hook. Outside, the sun was bright, hurting their eyes after the dimness of the brick, tomb-like building.

"We've done it! We're here! America!" Otto smiled broadly,

hugging Gretchen and Anna, pumping George's hand in a manly handshake.

"Where to now?" Gretchen asked.

"The ferry to New Jersey." George was searching for directions. "There, the ferry directory is over there," he pointed.

Thoughtfully, the word "ferry" was in English, Russian, German, French, and Italian with directional arrows to the city each served.

They pushed through the gathering, fortunately finding a vacant bench overlooking the bay. They sank down gratefully, the long two-hour ordeal behind them.

George idly leafed through the forms. Something caught his eye. He sat bolt upright.

"These papers are wrong! Look how they spelled our last name!" He pointed excitedly. "S-T-E-R-N, not 'Sternvald'! See, he wrote Papa's name as 'Stern, V. Otto.' He has made all of us 'Stern' for a last name! I'll go back in. I'll get it corrected."

George pushed back to the exit door and entered. A large, strong arm reached out, fixing him in his tracks. "You don't come in here!"

"I have to. Our papers."

"Look, nobody comes through this door. Now stay out!"

George contemplated the situation. He obviously could not gain entrance here. Walking to the side of the building, he saw a high fence with three strands of barbed wire running from the building across the yard, down the steep bank and out several feet into the water. No gate or opening could be seen. He saw people moving about outside the main entrance and more disembarking from a recently docked liner. Even if he could get back, he would never get through the crowd today. He stood, thinking. Jan and Jared's captain would probably know what to do. Surely there must be a way to solve this, an emigration office in New Jersey or New York, perhaps. He went back to his family and explained their predicament and his proposed solution.

"I see no other reasonable answer," Otto said finally. "We'll attend to this problem later as George suggests. For now let's find our ferry."

They left the ferry at the terminal near the north end of Jersey

City and walked a short two blocks to a small restaurant. They were escorted to a window table by a pleasant waitress and were handed menus, and they set their hand luggage nearby under Gretchen's watchful eye.

Moments later the restaurant door burst open and three young men in uniform entered, laughing and joking with each other.

"Jan, over here," George called out.

"Well, well, it's a small world after all." Jan walked to the table and sat down. "Everything alright? Do you have lodging?"

George detailed the name change problem they had encountered.

"I've heard it happens. The clerk just spells the name as he thinks it sounds and that's that," Jan said.

"You mean it can't be changed?" Gretchen asked in disbelief.

"Oh, I'm sure there's a way, but I don't know how."

"Your captain, maybe?" Otto interjected.

"Maybe," Jan said. He pushed his cap farther back on his head, then stood. "Look, I have to run. There's a comfortable family hotel up this street called the Atlantic Inn. You can get meals there, too. The ship is docked at Pier Seventy-four, at the foot of Harbor Street, and your belongings are being unloaded in the warehouse. Look, Jared is still on board. Go down this evening and ask for him. He can get you on to see Captain Borkgren. If the Captain can't help, he'll know who to see. I'll be off now, and again, good luck."

Having paid for their meals, they retrieved their luggage and walked to the Atlantic Inn. Anna trudged along, wrestling her suitcase with both hands. Finally George took pity on her and carried it the final block to the inn. They rented adjoining rooms near the back on the third floor. Unpacking and chatting about the day's events. It was decided Otto and George would visit the *Kongsberg* to seek the captain's aid.

Chapter 5

The sun had set; twilight lingered above the surrounding buildings. Streetlights blinked on, making the short four-block journey to the ship a pleasant interlude. The wharf was bustling with activity, and from all appearances, work would extend far into the evening. Heavy wagons carted the cargo from ship to warehouses. Giant cranes, either on the ships or moving along the rail tracks on the wharf, reached their arms into the bowels of the vessels, removing load after load of netted or crated supplies. The *Kongsberg* sat high in the water, the majority of tonnage now on the dock or under cover in one of the cavernous warehouse lining the waterfront.

Captain Borkgren, a slender, ruddy-complexioned man nearly as tall as George, listened to their story with interest and concern. Yes, he had heard of this happening before. Yes, there was a remedy, though time-consuming and burdened with governmental regulations and delays. Most people accepted the newly-bestowed surname provided by the imagination of an often uncaring public servant. However, should they wish, the nearest office of emigration was in New York City. The captain rustled about his desk and produced an U.S. Federal Bureaus guide. "Here's the address." He handed Otto a slip of paper containing the information.

"We appreciate the help, even though it may prove to be an effort in futility," Otto sighed. "Come, George. Let's share this news with your mama, then to dinner and early bed. Have to see the bank in the morning, get train tickets, and arrange the shipping of our goods west."

"Good-bye," the captain said. "Maybe someday I will eat one of your apples when I'm in port in Seattle."

"Good night, Captain," George said. "Give our best to Jan and Jared."

"Let's hurry along, your mother will be fretting," Otto called back as he started down the gangplank.

"Just a minute, I'll be right with you." George paused, glancing about, thinking back over the last few days and the enjoyment of the trip. He started to follow but noted Otto was not waiting at the bottom of the gangplank near the night-light. Then he saw his father spread-eagle on the dock, arms extended, one leg bent grotesquely under him. Sailors and longshoremen had gathered near the body, several shaking their heads in disbelief, then turning away. One appeared ready to vomit.

When the captain closed his door, Otto had been momentarily without light. Suddenly enveloped in darkness, he lost his sense of direction. His next step was into emptiness. The waist-high guard chain provided no protection as he hurtled out and down. The metal corner of a loading crane received the full impact of Otto's head and body, the collision tearing away the left side of his skull and face, as a dulled axe would sever a melon. He was dead when his somersaulting body smashed onto the wooden planking of the wharf.

"Papa!" The young voice rose above the noise of the harbor, its despair and agony reverberating between the ships and buildings.

Chapter 6

Anna and Gretchen heard a knock at the door.

"Good," Gretchen said. "Your papa and George must be home. I was getting worried."

Anna skipped to the door, flinging it open, ready to throw her arms around Papa. She drew back, startled. A young man in uniform stood there instead. The dimness of the hallway precluded Anna recognizing Jared for a moment.

"Oh, hello, Jared." She turned. "Mama, it's Jared from the ship."

"How nice. We didn't expect to see you again. Otto and George aren't home yet."

"May I come in, Ma'am?" Without waiting for an answer, Jared stepped into the room and politely removed his cap, his face ashen, a tremor in his speech. "Could we sit down, please?"

Gretchen motioned to a chair, then sat in the matching chair next to him.

Anna came and stood beside her mother expectantly as Jared turned his hat nervously between his fingers, looking from one to the other.

"I'm afraid I have some very bad news," Jared said, then blurted out, "Otto is dead."

Gretchen started to rise, then slumped back. Anna's posture became rigid. Neither spoke.

"This cannot be." A long pause followed. "A mistake, yes?" Gretchen beseeched.

Jared cleared his throat. "No, Ma'am, no mistake I'm afraid." He looked down at the floor, his cap and hands now stilled.

The silence was stifling. Jared's words struck Gretchen as a knife:

sharp, burning, unrelenting. *Otto dead?* Not the sweet boy who arrived so handsome and innocent at their front door at age seventeen seeking a summer job then stayed on to rebuild the farm back to her father's dream. Later, he stood rock-solid as they watched ill health render her father a helpless invalid until death's kiss. The man who stood before her naked and wet from a torrential storm, undressing her, taking her tenderly and gently into womanhood in the soft bed under the eaves, the storm within more demanding than that outside? Not Otto! Gone his understanding, patience, strength, manhood, fatherhood, and wisdom? Gone by the mere utterance of a few words by a young man slightly older, perhaps, than the son they had spawned in love and need? No, it had not happened; this was a bad dream from which she would wake. A nightmare thrust upon her by that cruel, uniformed young man who sat before her. They could not take her Otto. She would not let him die.

"And George?" Gretchen asked quietly, almost as an afterthought.

"Fine. He's fine. He's with the police on the docks. He'll be home soon, I'm sure."

Gretchen glanced about the unfamiliar room, pulling Anna tight against her. Suddenly George raced into the room, moved to his mother's side and sank to his knees in front of her. Gathering her and Anna in his arms, he hugged them tightly, the three bodies moving as one, sobbing, swaying, George finally pulling back. He made a vain effort to wipe away his tears and sweat with his already damp shirtsleeve.

"I sent Jared on ahead," George said. "I didn't know now long the police would detain me. Thank you, Jared, for coming."

Jared nodded, saying nothing. Slowly the threesome regained a sense of composure.

"How was... how did your father... ?" Gretchen could not continue.

George pieced together the facts as best he could but left out the detail about Papa's head.

"I must go to him," Gretchen said, getting up briskly. "Now where did I leave my handbag? Your father will be upset if I leave it behind." She moved about the room as one preparing to go grocery shopping.

Her voice had no trace of concern or sadness. "Is it chilly out? Of course it is. Silly me." George and Anna could not believe her actions. Were the actions affected, a front for their benefit? "Oh, here it is." She retrieved her handbag from the dresser. "And my shawl." She threw it across her shoulders with a flourish and turned to the others. "Well, shall we be off?"

George exchanged frightened glances with Anna. Jared stood up, uncertain whether to flee or linger, on the vague chance he may still be of help. "Mama!" George jumped up, blocking her exit to the door. "I think you should stay here. All that can be done for now has been done."

Gretchen and George's eyes met. He saw hers were glassy, unfocused. Even in the relative brightness of the room, her pupils were fully dilated. He reached out, grasping her shoulders firmly.

"Mama!" he repeated. "Do you hear me?"

She stood, apparently not comprehending, her eyes darting about as a bird's in a futile attempt to extricate itself from a snare.

He shook her, almost brutally. "Look at me! Answer me!"

"George, what can we do?" Anna fell on the bed, sobbing.

"Be still, Anna!" George said, "Can't you see—"

"Don't speak to your sister like that, George!" Gretchen's voice was harsh and authoritative. "Your father, your father... ," her voice faltered, "God! Oh, God! Your father is dead." The last words a near whisper. Anna watched in alarm as without warning her mother went limp in George's arms, sinking to the floor, the handbag landing at her feet. George managed to catch her, lifted and carried her to the bed. He turned. "Jared, one last favor?"

Jared nodded his consent.

"Find the landlady and tell her we need a doctor. Hurry, please!"

"Right away." Jared rushed out.

Gretchen lay motionless on the bed, eyes closed. George moved to Anna's side. He held her close, strong arms encircling her slender, sob-shaken form. "I promise I'll never let anything happen to you. Cry, let it out. We will need to be strong for each other. And Mama will need us both, now more than ever." They clung together, not knowing what the future held.

Before long, a doctor, accompanied by the owner of the inn, arrived. After introductions and a brief recap of the evening's events, the doctor conducted a brief examination of Gretchen.

"Shock," the doctor said. "She's resting now, and that's good." He removed a small packet from his black bag. "Give her two of these tonight, and one every night until the supply is exhausted."

George pressed some money into the doctor's hand, thanked him, then closed the door softly behind as the owner and doctor departed, discussing the situation in low, concerned tones.

George roused Gretchen long enough to force two pills and cool water down her throat. Protesting slightly, she soon drifted off. George placed a warm blanket over her feet and upper legs, dimmed the lights, and with Anna moved to the adjoining bedroom. Tired and exhausted, he fell into a deep sleep. Anna lay beside him, sobbing. Then, legs drawn up in a fetal position, she, too, slept.

Chapter 7

The next few days were interspersed with bouts of intensive arguments, confusion, accusations, sadness, forgiving and misgivings between Gretchen and George. He remembered it as a time of great turmoil, the strong fabric of his family bond shredded and tattered, poorly patched, never renewed to its former self. Mama the unraveler; he the tailor seeking in vain to restore the familiar pattern. Through it all, George was Anna's anchor. She felt safe harbor when his arms and reassuring words embraced her, protecting her from the storm raging about them. She would never forget as long as she lived.

"We'll be going home, of course," Gretchen said one morning, dipping her toast in hot coffee. "Back to Germany."

"You can't mean that, Mama," George said.

"Oh, yes I do. I'll take Anna home. You can run off into the wilds like your Uncle Hans. Good riddance."

"Mama!" Anna said, starting to whimper.

"We must stay together as a family. It was Papa's wish and I promised I would be there to help." George said.

"So, now you are the man of the house?"

"Yes, now that Papa is gone. I have control of the money and the tickets. Besides, I can make it work; we can be together as a family should."

"Without Papa we are no family."

"Without Mama we are not either," he said gently.

"Please say we can stay," Anna said, "please."

"No."

"Then I will stay with George," Anna said firmly.

"So that is how it is. You turn my own daughter against me."

"No, it is her choice."

"You will regret this, both of you. I have no husband and now no children," she said with a bitterness that made them shudder. "You young fool!" Gretchen flared at George. "You are not Otto now—you will never be Otto. You are a stupid, arrogant pup. What a disappointment you would be to your father, strutting about like the cock of the walk! No, never can you take your father's place!"

Her words hurt George deeply. He wanted to strike back with words of his own, tear at her heart as his heart was so badly wounded. What strengths he had gained the last days where badly eroded. Where a small sense of pride was emerging had now been nearly destroyed. This charge of his inability to be like his father would be a driving force within him the rest of his life. *I must keep the family together, but at what price?* George thought remorsefully.

They argued about the funeral arrangements, Gretchen insisting Otto be sent back for internment in Weserburg. "But Papa's grave shouldn't be thousands of miles away from us," George protested. Begrudgingly, she agreed to cremation and taking the ashes with them. The funeral parlor presented the remains in a small, sturdy wooden box with secure locking devices on either side. A plain brass plate was attached to the face of the container: "Otto Karl Sternvald, beloved husband and father, 1871-1908."

There was no church service, no minister. Plans to visit the New York Emigration Headquarters were forgotten. Efforts to change the name back to Sternvald would be postponed, at least for the present. George made the necessary visits to the Mellon Bank and the storage depot, arranging for transfer of funds to the local bank in Aurora and the forwarding of their belongings by rail car. The least expensive was via the Chicago and Eastern Rail Company, then transfer at Chicago to a local spur line into Saint Paul, Minnesota. From there, connections west on the Great Northern Railroad to the railhead in Seattle, Aurora being a scheduled stop en route. *Is this what you would do, Papa?* George asked himself.

Six days following Otto's death, a coroner's inquest had been held in the Jersey City Municipal Building. Gretchen refused to attend, which was just as well. The hearing was brief and to the point. Statements from Captain Borkgren and Jared were read into the record; a deputy coroner gave a brief but graphic account of Otto's body and cause of death; two policemen gave their testimony and that of several others who chanced to eyewitness the tragedy. Finally George was asked to relate his version of that evening's events. Fifteen minutes later a verdict of "accidental death" was rendered, the file stamped, "Closed." The case of Otto V. Stern, a.k.a. Otto Karl Sternvald, completed

When George returned to the inn, Gretchen was sitting near the window. Anna sat across the room, leafing idly through the pages of an old magazine, her favorite doll wedged between her and the arm rest. Gretchen's hair was uncombed, its sheen dulled by lack of attention, her clothing and body pungent with the odor of neglect. George moved to her side and bent to kiss her cheek. She drew away. George sighed and walked to Anna, squatting down so he was level with her face.

"Anna."

"Yes, George?" She glanced up.

"All the arrangements are made except getting the train tickets. I pick them up this afternoon. If all goes well, we can be on our way tomorrow or the day after."

Anna closed the magazine, then looked across to the silent figure of her mother. "What will we do about Mama? She eats so little. She won't talk, or when she does she's so angry... and mean." Tears welled in her eyes.

"Look," George said softly, taking Anna's hands in his, "things will work out. I can be with you and Mama most of the time now. Be patient just a day or so more?"

"I'll try."

"I love you, Wee One. You've been so strong and brave. I don't know how I could have managed without you." He hugged her. She clung to him for a moment, placing a soft kiss on his whiskered cheek.

"I guess I should shave," George noted, rubbing his hand across his youthful whiskers. "We have to convince Mama to get out of those clothes and take a bath," he said softly.

"I've tried, she pushed me away and told me to leave her alone. I was scared."

"Well, I'm here now, and whatever it takes, Mama will have to cooperate. We can't have her going on the train looking and smelling like that." George crossed the room and stood in front of his mother. Pulling himself to his full six-foot, one-inch height, he announced in his deepest voice:

"Mother, get up. You are to get out of those clothes and take a bath now."

Gretchen looked up at him, smiling. "Yes, my darling, yes, of course. I must look nice for my Otto."

"Anna will help you. Go in the other room and undress. Anna, draw your mother a bath."

Slowly, but with resolve, Gretchen walked to the adjacent room and carefully undressed, then moved to the bathroom and the warm, restful water. Almost lightheartedly Gretchen applied the wash cloth to her neck and face. "Otto should be along soon. I want to look my best." She hummed a tune as she cleaned and rinsed her hair, then lay back to soak a few minutes. "I have something I must tell him. I can't remember what it is. Oh well..."

They left the Jersey City Terminal two days later. Although the extended delay and unexpected cost of Otto's death had made inroads into their cash reserve, the funds from the sale of the farm were still undisturbed. Due to Mama's mental condition and her desire to be away from others, George opted to spend additional money required to procure a small stateroom en route to Aurora. The trip west was uneventful. For the most part, George and Anna sat watching the landscape flash by or observed people at the various stops along the way. Gretchen seemed uninterested and unconcerned. Except for an occasional visit to the bathroom, she seldom left the confines of the room. Meals, usually half eaten if at all, she took in their compartment.

George and Anna talked of the enormity of the vast countryside, the soaring mountain range of the Rockies as the train pushed across

Montana into Idaho, then Spokane, Washington. Aurora was five hours away; Anna and George could scarcely hold back their joy. Across the dry, desolate plains of Eastern and Central Washington the train sped. Occasionally a large dryland wheat ranch was seen dotting the horizon. Clumps of trees and the rooftops of a house and outbuildings revealed homesteads of hearty pioneer settlers. Nearing journey's end, the tracks paralleled the Columbia River, then crossed to the river's west bank on a high, single-track trestle, then followed the river into the village of Aurora.

Nearly two months had elapsed since they had boarded the river barge at Weserburg... a journey started with such high hopes and dreams, now shattered; a future unknown.

George turned to Anna and Mama. "We're home!"

"Come, Mama, we must get off now," Anna said.

Gretchen rose, a look of excitement across her face. The children noticed and took heart.

"George," Mama turned to him, "don't you try to carry all the bags. Let Papa help you."

"Yes, Mama," George said gently.

Anna took Gretchen's hand and led her to the stairs and onto the platform. The air was warm, an Indian summer, October 23, 1908.

Chapter 8

George Stern lay on his back, eyes half-closed, arms folded comfortably across his bare chest. His well-worn work pants were faded to near white in spots; one pant leg, partially ripped from an encounter with a barbed fence months ago, clung to his strong, muscled leg. The hum of the warm summer afternoon lulled him deeper into his mood. He thought of kicking off the heavy, dirt-stained boots and surrendering to sleep.

"George!"

He rolled his head slowly in the direction of his wife's voice, the tall orchard grass obscuring his vision. He raised his head slowly, resting it on his large, work-roughened hand.

"Over here, Sarah!" he shouted. George waved his right arm back and forth as a signal. He could hear her coming, long skirt swishing against the lush groundcover.

"So, lazybones, this is how you get a heavy day's work done?" She came and stood over him, hands on hips in mock anger.

"Don't nag me, old woman," he said, pulling her gently to the grass beside him. Sarah lay looking up at George, eyes sparkling with the happiness of the moment; they lay sharing the love each had for the other.

He kissed her gently and placed his cheek against her silky one. "I love you, old woman."

"And I, you," Sarah answered, her hands kneading the muscles of his shoulders with tenderness.

His hand moved along her side, seeking a small, high breast beneath her blouse. She did not resist, but arched her back slightly to meet the caress.

"Not now, dearest," she murmured.

He stopped with an unhappy sigh. Patting her on the rear, he rolled over and up to his feet. Reaching down, he took her hands as she bounded to a standing position, then brushed off the dry grass and leaves clinging to her gray skirt.

"Mama!" a small child's voice called from across the orchard.

"Oh, dear, that's Gina. I have to run. See you at supper." Sarah hurried off. "Mama's coming, Gina!" she called out. George watched her go, body young and slender, the sun bouncing off her deep auburn hair that hung nearly to her waist when not pinned up. He strolled to a nearby tree, drawing a deep swallow of cool water from the glass jar he had placed in the shade at its base. Looking down the gentle slope of the orchard, the river beyond, he was reminded of his childhood home in Germany. With reluctance, he turned to thinning the trees of the small green apples, deftly selecting the smaller ones for discard on the ground, careful also that the space between the remaining fruit allowed maximum growth for harvest in the fall. Working steadily, he completed several rows of apples before checking his pocket watch, once his father's, and saw it was nearing six p.m.

The evening sun was kissing the peaks of the Aurora Mountain Range as George headed for the house, his twelve-hour workday complete. He opened the screen door and entered the kitchen. The room was hot from the day and heat of the cook stove despite the two open windows, which provided some degree of cross ventilation.

"Dinner should be ready in a few minutes."

George noted the dampness on Sarah's forehead and the delicate beads of perspiration on her upper lip. He gentled them away with his finger then softly brushed his lips to hers.

"Where's Gina?"

"She was bored, so I sent her off to town with Anna. She took the Ford into town to run a few errands for me. They should be back any minute now."

The alarmed cry of the hens signaled the arrival of the small touring car as it bumped and chugged its way over the rutted, dusty driveway, then came to an abrupt halt under the summer apple tree near the barn. A cloud of dust engulfed the car momentarily, then dispelled across the side yard. Peals of laughter and unrestrained giggles were heard as Anna and Gina appeared from the last lingering dust cloud and made their way across the yard toward the back door. Anna carried two large sacks, Gina a smaller one.

During dinner the family chatted about the day's activities. Later, table cleared and the dishes put away, they retired to their rooms; Anna read Gina to sleep before she to fell asleep reading in her own room. George reviewed a supply list while Sarah completed some darning and mending of clothes. It was past dark when they turned down the bed light and went to sleep.

Chapter 9

FIVE YEARS LATER

George and Sarah and family had moved from the Homeplace to a fine new home in town. One evening, prior to going home, George made his weekly visit to the hundred acre Homeplace. He had been fortunate in finding an excellent operator to manage the ranch on a day to day basis. William "Billy" Halladay, his wife Fran, and their four sons lived there year-round. The orchard, house and outbuildings showed excellent care, thanks to the dedicated efforts of the Halladay family.

The last apple boxes had been collected, tree props placed in neat piles at various locations between tree rows. The final fall watering completed, the long, busy hours of harvest now behind them. The trees stood naked of the bountiful crop awaiting the winter cold that drove the sap into the trunk and roots for the dormant season. Pruning would not start until late January or mid-February depending on weather conditions.

"Place looks real good, Billy," George said, having found his foreman at work in the equipment shed. They chatted about matters pertaining to upkeep, repairs and the costs from a list Billy had prepared; George reviewed the list, asked a couple questions and approved the requests. Satisfied, as usual, with the efforts Billy had achieved, he bade good-bye and drove home.

Gorge had retired to the library of the new family home, Ridgemont, to review some financial statements, while Sarah sat in the living room, hemming the bottom of a new skirt she had purchased. The flapper look required the knee be exposed to be "in style." At her age, despite her youthful appearance and long, slender legs, she felt a little foolish. Gina was sitting close by, turning the pages of the photograph albums Sarah had set aside during the day's housecleaning.

"Mama?"

"Yes, dear?"

"I don't know some of these people in the pictures. Could you tell me who they are?"

"Give me a few more minutes to finish and then I can."

Gina sat patiently watching as Sarah deftly pushed the needle in and out of the material, using the silver thimble on the end of her third finger to add pressure to the needle's entry.

"There." Sarah stood up, holding the skirt against her, extending one leg to test where the hemline hit. "Oh, dear, still a little high. It will show half my thigh when I sit down."

"It's so pretty, and you'll look so beautiful in it, Mama. May we look at the albums now, please?"

Mother and daughter snuggled against the high-backed upholstered davenport, the books on Gina's lap. She opened to the first page of the large hand-tooled, leather-bound album. "Here," Gina said, pointing to a picture of a man in his fifties holding up a forty-inch-long salmon. "Is that Grandpa Fox?"

"Yes."

"Is that you with him?"

"No, dear, that was my mother."

"She looks so young... I mean compared to Grandpa." It was a half-question, half-observation.

"Yes, she was much younger. You see, your grandpa married late, mainly because he traveled about so much and loved to be involved in adventure. As an example, when he was fifteen he went to California with the thousands that came to find gold."

"Did he find gold? Was he rich?" Gina asked expectantly.

"No, nothing as exciting as that, but he did make considerable money buying and reselling supplies and tools to the gold miners from his supply wagon. With that money he bought land near San

Francisco which later made him more money."

"Then he was rich!" Gina said.

"Well, not rich exactly," Sarah said with a laugh. "Besides, he lost most of it when he bought into a sailing ship that sank with a full cargo—at least that's what he was told. Years later, he found the ship's captain had sold the supplies in San Diego, sold the ship, and skipped to Mexico with the money."

"So what did he do then?"

"He signed on as a deck hand and sailed for nearly three years. He had wondrous stories to tell of China, India, Australia, South America. He came home to San Francisco in 1858, just in time to hear of the gold fever on the Fraser River in British Columbia. He caught the next ship out and followed the mining camps from British Columbia into Idaho and Montana."

"But when did he marry Grandma?" Gina asked, somewhat impatiently.

"I'm coming to that. Grandpa Fox had saved his money and worked hard, hauling supplies and selling them, just as he had done during the California gold rush. Well, he decided to make his home in Seattle. It was very small then, about 3,500 people, the size Aurora is today. Your grandpa saw the potential growth in the area so he bought land near Puget Sound and on the outskirts of Seattle. Then he made money—a lot of money."

"Then he was rich?" Gina asked.

"Yes, then he was rich." Sarah smiled.

"And then he married Grandma?"

"Yes. Grandpa was fifty, but he didn't look it except for his white hair. He met and married a young schoolteacher named Martha Wiseman. There was quite a fuss, I guess, her being only twenty-four and all, marrying this old man when so many young men were around."

"Maybe she married Grandpa 'cause he was rich!"

Sarah smiled at Gina's girlish wisdom. "That may have had something to do with it, but I believe they were also very much in love. I know your grandfather was deeply in love with her. They were married in April, eighteen eighty-six, in a small church near Queen Anne Hill. He later built a beautiful home overlooking the Sound in the area now known as Magnolia. Sadly, your grandmother died in August the next year."

"What happened, Mama?"

"She died giving birth, giving birth to me. She bled to death right in the hospital, and they could do nothing to save her. Oh, God, how many times I've wished it had been me that died and not her." Sarah's eyes brimmed with tears, her mouth trembled.

"Don't cry, Mama. I'm sure you didn't know."

"That's what Daddy said over and over. But it's like a stone inside me sometimes. I doubt if I'll ever get over it." Sarah looked away, then back at the pictures, her hand gently resting on her mother's face, then her father's. "I'm sorry, Daddy," she murmured, choking back a sob. She sighed, regaining her composure.

Gina sat uncertain what to say or do. She turned the page.

"Is this Papa? He looks so funny in that hat."

Sarah brightened. "Yes, that's your father standing with Rosemary, the horse he rode when he was the ditch rider for the Irrigation Company. That's how I first met your father, as a matter of fact, during his ditch riding days." She was laughing now, the memories of her courtship flooding back.

"Tell me about it, Mama," Gina begged.

"I've told you the story before."

"I know, but tell me again, tell me the first time you met Papa." Gina giggled, knowing what was to come.

"Well, if you insist." Sarah reached and stroked Gina's happy face. "And then to bed with you."

"I promise," said Gina delightedly.

"After Mama died, Grandpa just wasn't the same anymore. I don't remember, of course, I was only a baby, but other people told me. During the next year he sold most of his holdings and decided to move out of the house and out of the town that held so many fond, but now sad memories. To make a long story short, he chose to move to Aurora and retire. He bought the Homeplace, built the house, ran a few cattle down by the river. There wasn't the irrigation canal then, of course. Later on, when there was water, he planted one of the first large orchards in the valley."

"What about meeting Daddy?" Gina asked, fidgeting with the tassels on the edge of the cushions.

"Your father, his mother, and Auntie Anna had moved to Aurora in the fall of nineteen aught-eight. The irrigation ditch had only been in a few years, and land was still available. The Sterns bought fifteen acres right next to us—the Wickford place. Wickford didn't know beans about farming and was about to lose it anyway. Your father made over the run-down barn into a house before winter set in. Poor dear had to haul water from the river the first winter. That spring the Irrigation Company was looking for a ditch walker, and they hired this tall, handsome, broken-English-speaking boy for the job. It must've been his smile. Since the job required only half a day's time, your daddy could spend the other half working the ranch. And did it need work."

"Come on, Mama, get to the good part," Gina persisted.

"It was late spring, maybe early summer. No, I remember now, it must have been mid-June."

"Mama!" Gina said, frustrated at her mother's delay.

Sarah giggled. "You think I'd forget the day I met your father? Not likely. It was June 22, 1909, at about eleven-thirty in the morning. I had been picking asparagus along the back edge of the orchard—it was a hot, hot day for that time of year. I found myself by the ditch bank; the water looked so cool and inviting, I decided to take advantage of the opportunity.

"I took off my dress and shoes and...," she looked at her daughter, "and my bodice—"

"Mama!" Gina interrupted. "You never told me that before!"

"Hush, child." Sarah giggled again. "Yes, my bodice—I still had my underpants on. I slipped into the canal and was having a wonderful time splashing about, jumping up and down, and cooling off. Suddenly a shadow was on the water. Without thinking I turned around, and there was your father, sitting on Rosemary, watching me make a darn fool of myself."

"What did you do?" Gina was more excited.

"Wasn't much I could do. Ducked down in the water, of course, and tried to cover myself up."

"What did he say? What did he do?" Gina asked, her voice excited, eyes wide with anticipation.

"Well, let's see." Sarah could remember as if it were yesterday. "He said, 'Good morning, Madam,' in his broken English—he had quite an accent then. 'How is the fishing today?' Then, he got down off the horse and came down the bank to the water's edge and knelt there! 'Hot day,' he said to me as if nothing was wrong. I was mad and embarrassed. He took off that silly hat and shaded his eyes, looking at me. Then he ran his fingers through the water, gentle-like, making small waves, and said, still looking straight at me, understand, 'Water runs very clear this time of the season. I can see the bottom with no trouble at all.' Then he grinned that handsome grin of his and kinda ambled back to his horse, as if he had all the time in the world. I was getting cold now, but I had to stay under water up to my neck.

"'It was very nice seeing you,' he said. 'Perhaps I'll see you again?'

"When he spoke he emphasized the word 'see.' Oh, I was so embarrassed. Then he said, 'By the way, my name is George Stern, Miss Fox. Please give my regards to your father.' He rode off, slowly, still looking and grinning."

"I love that story." Gina smiled up at her mother. "What happened next?"

"And the next day it rained," Sarah said.

"What?" Gina wrinkled her nose and brow, not understanding.

"Oh, it's something my father used to say when he didn't want to tell me more stories and I was begging him to go on, just as you are now."

"But you and Daddy saw each other again."

"Yes, silly. We got married four years later."

"Tell me about it, please."

"Some other time. Now off to bed with you. It's getting late. Skedaddle now." Sarah gave Gina a friendly swat on her bottom.

Gina skipped out of the room and up the stairs. Sarah gathered up the albums and set them aside, deciding she would have to go through them soon. Skirt and darning basket in hand, she climbed the stairs to tuck Gina into bed.

"Going to bed so soon?" George's voice startled her from her errand. He stood at the bottom of the stairs, a glass of milk in one hand, sugar cookies in the other.

She placed a finger on her lips. Speaking in a low stage whisper, she said, "No, just seeing that Gina is tucked in, then I'll be back down."

In the living room George noticed the albums lying near the sofa. Sitting down, he began thumbing through the pages, the pictures recalling so many memories. While the majority of the pictures were dominated by the Fox ranch house on the Homeplace, his attention was drawn to a small, faded photograph. Beside the house, partially in shadow, stood four people in a stiff, holding-still-for-the-camera pose. He studied the picture carefully. Opening the drawer of the small table next to the sofa, he removed a round reading glass with a grooved black handle. "That's better," he said half-aloud, as the faces jumped into focus. He stood on the left, then Sarah, Anna, and his mother. Carefully removing the picture from the triangular fasteners, he turned it over, seeking a date. There was none. He turned it back over. Leaning close to gain the benefit of the side lamp, he again studied the faces intently. He grinned, looking at himself, tall and awkward in his high, stiff-starched collar and the ill-fitting Montgomery Ward catalog suit. Sarah, smiling and slender, wearing a long, simple frock, form-fitting and high-necked but with fullness in the skirt. Anna, smiling as usual, was dressed in a white blouse, a dark skirt at mid-calf, and stockings. Mama—how old she looked for her age—her face placid but unsmiling, an outdated dress brought from Germany hanging on her once-handsome figure.

"I sorted those out today," Sarah said, reentering the room. "I plan on putting some in the library, some in the attic." She walked closer, looking down at the picture in her husband's hand.

George looked up. "Do you know when this was taken?" He handed the picture to Sarah.

She studied it for a moment. "Nineteen-fifteen. Remember? We moved into the Homeplace after father went to the rest home. Your mother died that spring, a God-sent blessing." Sarah sat down next to George, taking his hand and squeezing gently.

"True. She was never the same after that night we docked in New Jersey." They talked a little longer then hand in hand, mounted the stairs to bed.

Chapter 10

Anna had stopped by the house the following afternoon. After passing pleasantries, she begged off a dinner invitation, claiming a splitting headache, and drove away in her car. She had nowhere she wanted to go nor anyone she wanted to be with but soon was on the highway, headed in the general direction of the Homeplace. Topping the hill just outside town, she pulled onto a seldom-traveled county road until she reached a scenic point commanding a view of the entire valley. She turned off the noisy engine, set the hand brake and walked to the front of the car.

The radiator hissed steam from the overflow vent, then fell silent. Although mid-October, spring-like breezes tugged at the edge of her mid-thigh dress, the tassels caressing her shapely legs. She dared not wear such attire in her classroom, but weekends belonged to her as long as she was reasonably careful. Tucking the dress under her legs, she eased onto a front fender, insuring her balance by grasping the nearest headlamp mounted near the radiator. In the distance, taller peaks of the Cascades showed a cap of new snow. Nearby hills were dry-brown and tan, the shadows coloring the ravines a deep, rich chocolate. Here and there, firs and pines clustered in small groups while other stood alone, as if a sentinel on the perimeter of small war camps. The dusty-green orchard leaves, some with red-touched edges, hung limply from their branches, a few already dead beneath the tree. Small fires of flaming sumac and oak signaled a last hurrah before surrendering to a winter's kill.

Sliding from the fender, she walked to the rear of the car, the dry grass snapping under her shoes. Just beyond, the muted greys and greens of the scrub sage fought the breeze, whistling. Far to the right, near the bend of the Little Chief River where sandbars rode the tranquil current like dirty, misshapen barges sat the Homeplace. She saw the four poplar trees which guarded the corners of the farmhouse, a few yellowed leaves still clinging, others letting go, swirling in the wind to pile high against the huge trunks or cover the still green grass. Beyond the drive were the barn, machine shed, and other outbuildings, their dull red coats adding to the fall colors. Along the south property line, she glimpsed the faint tracks of the water-wagon trail—the trail her mama had apparently walked that last, fateful evening.

Anna shuddered, closing her eyes against the vision of her mother's body floating face-down, moving slowly in and out, in and out, as the ripples of the small eddy pushed against her, her long, stringy white hair blanketing the water. Nearby, the box containing Papa's ashes lay open, half in, half out of the water, the contents gone, God knew where. What possessed Mama to go to the river one could only speculate. For years she had awoke near noon, eaten a meager meal—not really caring what was offered her by Anna—then, depending on the time of year, sought the rocker on the side porch or near the front window in the living room. Talking only in German, muttering, laughing at her own private humor, singing childhood folk songs in an off-key pitch, then falling silent for hours; but rocking, always rocking. George and Anna would lie awake at night, listening to the creak, creak of the chair against the wooden floor.

Anna opened her eyes. The wind had picked up, its freshness carrying the nip of the fall days. *God,* Anna thought, *I look so much like Mama. What guarantee have I of not becoming a vegetable, losing my sanity? How can I think of marriage or children if this is true?* Her body screamed for the touch of a man she could love and who could love her. She pushed the thought back. As a teacher and a writer—an unpublished writer, save for a few poems—she could live her life to a degree of fullness and not become a burden to a husband, or worse, to a son or daughter as her mother had. The wind rose higher, kicking up wind-devils on the far hillsides.

Starting the car, she backed around and headed to town. Another weekend had passed and school would occupy her time again. *I must get back to writing,* she told herself.

Chapter 11

The economic chaos, brought on in part by the stock market crash in October 1929, heralded extreme difficulties for the nation and the world. George had watched the decline in international trade, the over-extension of credit with the accompanying burst of industrial and agricultural growth as a harbinger of potential problems. The intrusion of the government into the farm support system, the failure of the railroads to develop a profitable yield on investment, or to resolve their labor disputes, had impacted the fruit and other industry through delays and walkouts. Reliance on the railroads to deliver the fresh fruit to the marketplaces was essential to preserving or expanding the apple industry. Fortunately, with new and better methods of storage and shipping, the impact was not as severe as it might have been.

During 1927 and 1928, George sold his stocks at a profit in excess of a quarter-million dollars. He was proud of his stewardship of the monies he had when first arriving in Aurora and more even, his management of the fortune inherited from Sarah's father. The funds, both personal and business, had been transferred to the strong, conservative Northwest Bank, headquartered in Seattle. In order to maintain an appearance of support for the local bank, he kept a small business account to draw weekly pay checks against the Homeplace at Aurora Valley Bank and Trust. Sarah also carried a small household account of a few hundred dollars.

George had made additional moves to consolidate their financial position. The last large block of timberland near Seattle was sold, the proceeds placed in government bonds. Unless the government collapsed, his funds were safe and drawing a reasonable return. The

Homeplace, which now included his initial 15 acres plus Fox's 80 and other adjoining land totaled 200 acres and had been free and clear for years. George had, over the last year, reviewed the holding carefully and made some bold decisions: Old Winesap trees were pulled and replaced with Red Delicious; the picking cabins received renovations as needed; a larger, more efficient spray pump was installed to service the orchards.

A review to establishing the best fruit sorting and packing line in the cold storage was carefully planned and carried out at the same time. Storage and refrigeration facilities received priority for initially cooling the fruit on arrival to the packing line, which extended the storage of packed boxes awaiting shipment, thus avoiding the cost of handling and repacking the fruit. If hard times were to come, as he was sure they would, George wanted the most cost-effective operation possible as well as liquidity for the long pull.

The stock market crash affected many individuals in the valley. Tom Crawford and Isaac Weston, produce brokers George had used for years prior to establishing his own marketing firm some years before, sustained tremendous losses. Unable to cover margin calls or sell the stocks they held outright without chance of profit, they plunged into deep debt. The mortgage payments on the extravagant homes, now worth less than half the appraised values, went unpaid; foreclosure was initiated. Likewise, their orchards were lost, voluntarily conveyed back to the bank. Pressed to pay unsecured personal and business operation loans, the C and W Produce Brokerage Company closed its doors, its excellent reputation in the eastern fruit markets gone. George weighed the prospects of providing financial aid to his former brokers, but felt the burdens too great and draining, with little or no chance of recovery. Bitterness against him was voiced by each, a reaction necessitated by their desire to place the hurt and blame somewhere other than where it actually lay— their greed and irrational desire for money and power. The tragic finale came when Tom Crawford placed a .45 caliber revolver in his mouth and pulled the trigger, having already killed his wife and three children as they slept in the now-deteriorating mansion. Isaac Weston abandoned his house and moved to California to live with his wife's parents on a small truck farm near Sacramento.

For months, George worked fifteen to eighteen hours a day, often seven days a week, the responsibility of maintaining the home and family life resting with Sarah. Billy Halladay, with the help of his family, continued to operate the Homeplace in his usual efficient manner. Orchard help was readily available, all thankful to have a roof over their heads and a small but steady income. Billy selected his work force carefully, weeding out the unknowledgeable or unwilling and sending them "packin'", as he called it.

Anna was fired from her teaching position, not for lack of effort or dedication but because she was single and a woman. "After all," as the school president so indelicately put it, " your brother can provide for you." He turned and left her classroom without a backward glance.

Sarah welcomed Anna back to the family home with open arms and a happy heart. "Am I glad you will be with me, Anna. I need a friend."

"And I'm glad to have a place to call home," Anna said, putting down her suitcases. From a more practical standpoint, Anna could help with the housekeeping and childrearing. Anna was bitter, but also looked upon the situation as an opportunity to seriously attack her desire to be a professional writer.

Chapter 12

The household and Homeplace in secure and trusted hands, George turned his full attention to a most pressing problem, the cold storage and packing plant. As a major producer and buyer of apples in the Aurora Valley, the need to harvest, store, and sell the fruit became paramount—especially the marketing. Because of the years of association with Tom Crawford and Isaac Weston, he was able to reopen many of the brokerage contacts previously serviced by the defunct C and W. Through letters, but mostly by telephone, he wheedled, cajoled, begged and pleaded with the wholesalers in the Midwest and New York to act as outlet for his products. At the same time, many of the smaller ranchers were being pressured by Yeager's bank to repay crop or mortgage advances. Some of the weaker, less productive ranchers failed. George met with those that he felt strongest and most capable of survival. He needed volume to continue operation. In return for their promises to use his packing, storage, and marketing facilities, he provided funds to reduce or pay off the bank loans. He gained four major advantages in doing so: continued volume of fruit; loyal, quality-oriented clients; the continuation of his packing and storage plant; and, most valuable of all, time.

To those ranchers he supported, the Northwest Bank advanced working capital, or in extreme cases crop payments, to lower the debt against their orchards. Unknown to the ranchers, George was guarantor on many of the bank loans. By careful selection George also purchased or assumed debts on other tracts, moving a trusted employee onto the property as foreman or retaining the former owner as manager, granting them an option to repurchase at a later date. This gave them incentive to work harder and produce the best.

"After all," as George told his wife, "who knows that ranch better than the man who works it every day?"

The local bank, owned by Roscoe Yeager closed its door in January 1931. George had made a concerted effort to have a branch of Northwest Bank locate in Aurora. His request was dismissed for various reasons, the strongest being their lack of desire to move across the mountains and branch into a small, economically depressed community. Without a bank, deposits lost, the valley was on the verge of panic. Something must be done quickly. George called a town meeting, urging all businessmen and ranchers to attend. Despite the bitter cold, a large throng gathered in the Grange Hall the following evening, some out of curiosity, and others in despair, anger, or fear. All were hoping for a small miracle.

George walked to the front of the room and onto the raised platform. Two large, potbellied stoves, one located at each end of the old wooden structure, succeeded in providing sufficient heat to ward off the chill of the room. All the chairs had been occupied long before the seven-thirty starting time, with late arrivals standing along the walls or across the back. Many wore heavy wool jackets, billed hats with earflaps, overalls or trousers, and boots of leather or rubber. Small puddles of moisture lay on the floor as the snow brought in on footwear melted and accumulated. The odor of wet wool permeated the confining room, making the air musty and foul. George paused for a moment, gathering his thoughts. He raised his arms above his head and with his hands motioned for quiet. The low chatter stopped, a few "ssshhh!'s" were heard supporting his request.

"Gentlemen, thank you for coming on such short notice and under such unpleasant weather conditions. I had hoped we could all learn something about banking tonight, but I see Mister Yeager chose not to attend." The room erupted into laughter, then clapping, a few boos. George patiently waited for the group to settle down again. "I know all of us have a horror story to tell," George continued, "and as much as we wish we could do something about the bank closing, the fact is we must move ahead with our lives."

"Easy for you to say!" a voice rose in the back. "You didn't lose everything you owed!"

I must be careful, what I say, what I do, he thought. He looked out across the room. "You're right, Jacob, I didn't lose everything, and I thank God and luck for that. Neither do I want you—any of you—to lose any more. What most of you have lost is money through hard, back-breaking effort. It hurts and you're angry, and I'm angry with you. Without you and without this valley, I, too, will lose everything. And damnit, I'm not ready to throw it all away yet!"

Before he could speak again, another voice shouted, "Talk's cheap. What're we going to do about it?" The crowd shifted uneasily, waiting for an answer.

"Let's look at certain facts. One, we don't have a bank anymore; two, we can't do business very long without a bank. Do we all agree with that?"

A chorus of "Yes!"

"Question then: would you be willing to support a new local bank?"

The response was not so strong this time. A few "Maybe's" and "I don't know's" filtered back. The crowd was uneasy now, talking among themselves.

"Listen, listen, please," George said calmly, his voice carrying the ring of command. "I pledge to you, God and the Governor willing, there will be a bank in Aurora within the month. I pledge before you all tonight, to place one quarter of a million dollars on deposit in that bank to be retained here and used for the betterment and future of this valley!" The audience was suddenly alive with discussion. "You with inventory, jobs, homes, orchards, anyone with a true need will receive help, not charity. You will have to pay it back, with interest, but you will be granted help if at all possible. I pledge you that on my word of honor!"

The room exploded in loud cheers and clapping. People rushed to the stage to shake his hand, slap him on the back, to shout words of thanks and encouragement.

Jacob sought George out, clasping his hand in a strong, vise-like grip. "Thanks, Mister Stern. I'm sorry if I spoke out of turn."

"Jacob, in one way or another we're all in this together, sink or swim. And don't ever be afraid to express your concerns if they're genuine."

George's voice rose. "Thank you, thank you all for coming." Turning back to Jacob, he said, "Maybe we can do some business soon if all goes well. All right?"

"Yes, sir, and thanks again."

The hall emptied quickly as those in attendance rushed to tell family and friends. George sagged to a chair, exhausted. *I've pulled it off. Now if I can deliver. Have I got work ahead of me!* he thought. The warning words of his father echoed back, "Be watchful of those who have money. I can not respect or trust a man with money; I know it came by ill-gotten means."

No, Papa, you're wrong. These are my friends; I will not desert them. I have already gained much more land and wealth than many others because of the money, and with that money I can now make good come from it. I've pledged my honor, Papa.

Sarah and George sat late into the night talking, sharing their thoughts and ideas of how best to accomplish the task that lay ahead. Finally in bed, George tossed and turned restlessly, the plans formulating as he lay beside his now-sleeping wife, his mind fighting off the invading need to rest, finally drifting into a dreamless, deep slumber.

Chapter 13

He awoke at eight, surprisingly refreshed. Bathing hurriedly, he dressed and went downstairs. Gina had left for school. Sarah and Anna were sitting in the dining room, talking in low, excited tones about the events of the previous evening.

He smiled and kissed each lightly on the forehead.

"I'm going to call Crain over at Northwest Bank and see if he can pull some strings to get me an appointment with the Banking Commissioner and maybe the Governor tomorrow." He poured a cup of coffee and retreated to the library to make his calls. "Phil! Thanks for taking my call. I have a big favor to ask of you, and it doesn't concern money—at least not your money."

George and Phil had developed an excellent business relationship, which was blossoming into a growing personal friendship as well. George reviewed in detail the events of the last few days; the meeting of last night and the pressing need for quick action by the state.

"I'll make a few calls and see what I can do," Phil said. "I'll get back to you one way or another this afternoon. You'll need a correspondent bank. Please include us in your considerations."

"I wouldn't have it any other way. I'll appreciate all the support I can get. Thank you for the offer."

The second call came from Crain late that afternoon. "Can you get over here tomorrow?"

"Yes."

"I've given the commissioner the pertinent facts, but there'll be a substantial number of forms to complete and probably an extended question and answer meeting. Better plan on two days, and bring your most current audited financial records." Phil Crain paused. "You know, these guys think you have a screw loose, starting a bank now. They want one of our corporate officers to testify to our experience with you and a commitment that we will serve as your correspondent. Now, I've prepared a letter to that effect, but they want oral substantiation also."

"You'll be there, so that covers that," George said.

"Sorry, I can't."

"Suggestions?" George asked.

"I've been working on it, that's why the call is so late." Phil said, "Charles Wesslin. He knows more about your situation than anyone else except me. You've dealt with him in my absences."

"Great idea, I look forward to working with him again. I'll be in Seattle tomorrow night. Please have Wesslin ready to go with me."

George had rested, occasionally sleeping during the six-hour trip. In addition to passengers, the train carried the U.S. Mail, railway express freight, and milk products. Once out of the eight-and-one-half-mile tunnel burrowed under the snow-covered Cascade Mountains, the train made numerous short stops at small villages and towns, Skykomish, Index, Gold Bar, Startup, Sultan, Monroe, and Everett, then turned south, following Puget Sound past Edmonds, Richmond Beach, and finally Seattle. The trip, while slow and sometimes frustrating to a hurried traveler, could be made pleasant. George sat in the last car of the train facing the large plate-glass window and watched the grandeur of the towering mountains, tree-choked valleys, the streams, rivers and falls coursing through and down the landscape. Dropping down nearer the coast, the mountains gave way to the gentler, rolling hills still mantled with tall fir, pine, and cedar. Finally, across the flat coastal plain, here and there the land dotted with dairy herds, cattle, field crops, hay, and alfalfa. Barns and homes, clustered beneath groves of tall cottonwood, poplar, oak, chestnut or evergreen, surrounded by white fencing or barbed wire strung between cedar posts. Regardless of the time of year, the trip offered the traveler a kaleidoscope of colors and ever-changing scenes.

Charles Wesslin was at the King Street Station in Seattle to meet

George when he arrived.

They walked through the iron gates leading to King Street, and to a waiting taxi. "Any more news from Olympia?" George asked as they moved through traffic.

"We believe the charter will be granted without a great deal of trouble. Mister Crain convinced Mister Rockhurst, our Board Chairman, to call the Governor on your behalf. The meeting is set for tomorrow at eleven o'clock. We've been assured it's only a formality, but we still must go through the application process."

"What're the requirements regarding bank officers?" George asked.

"I presume you will be president?"

"Yes."

"You'll also be required to have a designated Secretary and a Cashier. Since you own the bank, you're not required to have a board of directors."

"We need a board. It gives the community a feeling of confidence and ownership. Charles, my biggest problem may be a cashier. I don't know that much about the day-to-day operation of a bank."

"A cashier is important. Faith in a bank more often comes from the day-to-day contact with the staff than management. Let's discuss it on the trip tomorrow," Wesslin suggested.

Before going to his room George placed a call from the lobby telephone booth. "Phil. George. I have another favor to ask of you and the bank. I need Charles Wesslin as my employee for a while." He went on to explain the discussion he and Charles had concerning a competent cashier.

"Charles could handle the job, no doubt in my mind. As to letting him go for a while..."

"Phil, get permission from whoever you need and get back to me tonight. I must have a cashier by tomorrow morning."

It was nearing midnight when the phone rang. "Phil again, George. I called Charlie at home. We can't let you and your bank go under before it even gets started. You have Wesslin for now. He can resign his position with us as of tomorrow so you may appoint him as cashier should the charter be approved. I've cleared it with Rockhurst, our Chairman. Charlie is delighted at the opportunity to serve you and, indirectly, us. You have to be on your toes tomorrow, try and get some sleep."

Two days later, George returned to Aurora triumphantly, the bank charter in hand. Within the week Charles Wesslin followed, his family shortly after. The Freeland Bank opened its doors for business ten days after the meeting at the Grange Hall.

Chapter 14

In the spring of 1935, George planned his last marketing trip to the East Coast and Midwest. Improved telephone and teletype communications allowed the contacting, negotiating and selling of fruit to other regions of the United States and Canada almost routine. Orders, confirmations and manifests were sent on a few minutes' notice. George had gathered a small, but dedicated, group of salesmen and support staff in an office adjacent to his new cold storage and packing line, a facility served by a rail spur of the Great Northern Railroad. The older units on the Homeplace, while less frequently used functioned as backup, when needed.

At George's urging, Anna accompanied him on his trip to New York. She had worked industriously on her novel, feeling it now ready to present for publication, though her credentials were at best slim: two poems accepted by *The Ladies Home Journal* and a short story in a small Northwest periodical which ceased publication in less than a year.

The day they arrived in New York was warm and sunny. Similar, Anna thought, to a day in September long ago when she and George stood on the deck of a ship in New York Harbor, crying for joy at the wondrous sight of "the lady."

They took rooms at the Chancellor, a charming hotel, two blocks from Central Park on West Fifty-eighth, near Columbus Circle. A brisk walk put them in the heart of the Broadway Theater district and fine restaurants.

Anna's corner rooms were bright and spacious. She immediately set about unpacking her trunks. A double bed dominated the bedroom, but allowed space for a large, double closet, a chest of drawers, two upholstered chairs of blue with tiny white flowers, designed to match the bedspread, pillow coverings, and padded headboard. The entire suite was carpeted in rich wool of pale blue-grey to complement the slate walls and dark, deep blue draperies. The tiled bath was located on an inside wall with a deep tub with shower, basin, towel rack, medicine cabinet, and stool. The wall opposite the tub was mirrored from floor to ceiling in small individual panes.

The main sitting room was finished in pastels, mostly warm yellows and creams. A small fireplace, with an oval-framed mirror above, was flanked on either side by bookcases containing current periodicals, a Bible, and several well-selected novels of the time. To the north a larger building blocked her view, but she could see glimpses of Central Park across the rooftops to the east. George's suite was directly across the hall.

She kicked off her shoes, pushing her toes into the soft carpet, then flung herself backward on the bed. *What a relief to be free of the cramped train compartment and the smells of railroads for a while,* she thought.

Later, each having showered and napped, they enjoyed a light supper in the hotel dining room before strolling the few blocks toward Central Park. The evening was cool; a gusty wind prophesied a storm front moving in with its accompanying rainsqualls and boiling clouds. They hurried back, fortunate to escape all but a few large raindrops. They pushed into the welcome shelter of the lobby.

"Would you like a drink before we go up?" George asked.

"A white wine would be nice, thank you."

The dark wood and dim, subdued lighting gave the room a pleasant warmth. Each table contained a replica of a carriage lamp, a small candle inside reflecting the muted light in the mirror-lined walls. They selected a small corner booth, then placed their order with the bar man then visited about activities for the next day. They finished their wine and sat relaxed a few more minutes before George said, "Shall we?" nodding toward the exit. Anna gathered her gloves and purse. "Ready when you are."

They walked through the lobby, noting the darkness outside, the wind-lashed rain slanting against the large plate-glass windows. A street light struggled bravely to penetrate the gloom but managed only a small yellow puddle of light around its stanchion.

In her room, Anna turned on the small desk lamp, noticed the drapes were still open, and the room damp and chilly. She considered lighting the fireplace but opted to retire early and read in bed. The volumes in the bookcase beside the fireplace were few but well-chosen: Sinclair Lewis' *Arrowsmith*, Dorothy Parker's *Enough Rope*, Willa Cather's *One of Ours*, and F. Scott Fitzgerald's *The Great Gatsby*. Not wishing to begin the reading of another novel, she decided to continue Hemingway's *A Farewell to Arms*, which she had earlier retrieved from her smaller trunk and placed on her nightstand. She wished she could write in his style; it seemed to flow so naturally.

She pulled the heavy drapery across the windows, shutting out the tiny drafts of air seeping around the casements, muffling the hammering torrent blown by the now-unbridled gale. In the bedroom, she turned back the fresh sheets, fluffed the pillows, then climbed into bed. Her silk nightgown clung against her trembling frame, an uncontrolled shudder coursing through her body. She pulled the downy comforter to her chin, feeling its warmth spread. Warmer now, she sat up in bed and unfolded the Street Guide to New York City, found and marked the location of agents and publishers she wished to visit. As George had said, many were within a short distance of the hotel. She selected two major publishers and an agent for tomorrow's visits. She yawned, set her alarm for nine o'clock, turned off the light and rolled onto her side, allowing her tiredness to take control.

Chapter 15

George awoke at four twenty-five, showered quickly, then dressed in white shirt and grey pinstripe suit. It was still dark, but the first morning light shone behind the eastern horizon. The storm had vented its fury, leaving only soft vapors as a remembrance.

Downstairs, he made inquiry of the availability of show tickets from the sleepy night clerk. He ordered two tickets to Eugene O'Neill's comedy, *Ah, Wilderness*, now in its second season. Afterward, a late supper at his favorite restaurant, La Siena, would provide Anna the excitement of an evening on Broadway.

He arrived at the auction a few minutes before six and sought Tony Tassoni, greeting his friend with a handshake and bear hug.

"Hey, Georgio, how's my favorite apple man?" He slapped George on the back with his ham-hock hand, nearly sending George sprawling. "C'mon, I'll buy you a cup o' joe."

As they passed through the warehouse, Tony stopped periodically to inspect vegetables or fruit, yelling orders in English, sometimes Italian, sometimes a mix of both. They entered an office piled high with bills of lading, manifests, invoices, and checks. The small desk, chair, and file cabinets were virtually buried beneath the papers.

The rest of the morning went quickly. George visited several other wholesalers, renewing contacts. It was nearing noon when he headed back to the warehouse, waiting in the office for Tony, passing pleasantries with Tony's sister, Maria, the office manager.

They arrived at Big Mama's Restaurant with the rest of the noontime crowd. Tony pushed his way in, moving like a run-amuck tank. A small table came free, and Tony claimed it, ignoring the unhappy looks of two men in business suits. "You know either of those gents?" Tony asked.

George shook his head.

"Good, then screw'em. They can find another table. Let's get some service over here!" Tony yelled. As was his habit Tony ordered the meal. The soup came, hot and steaming. Tony ladled a portion for himself and George from the cast iron pot into two big white bowls, then tore large portions of bread from the loaf, placing squares of butter on the remaining piece before his next bite. Uncorking the wine bottle, he poured the contents rapidly into two glasses. "*Salud*!" He touched his glass to George's, then downed half its content in one swallow. Halfway into the meal, Tony spotted a familiar face across the room. "Hey, Gus!" he bellowed. "Over here."

Gus ambled over and sat down.

"Waiter!" Tony yelled. "Bring some more of everything. George Stern, this here is my cousin, Guido Carducci, but everyone calls him Gus."

"You in the wholesale business too?" George asked.

Tony and Gus exchanged glances. "No, Gus is what you might call self-employed."

Gus smiled, his grin showing the gold filling in a front tooth.

"What line of work?"

"How's your pasta, George? A little more sauce?" Tony asked, avoiding an answer.

George did not press, but ate while Gus and Tony talked family between mouthfuls of food. Gus was the equal to Tony in the eating department, he observed.

"Hold my place, I gotta take a leak." Gus pushed back his chair and strolled toward the rest rooms in the back.

"Did I say something wrong?" George asked.

"Hell no, he just don't like talkin' about his work. Don't worry."

"Must do pretty well, whatever it is. That suit must've set him back a hundred bucks, tailor made if I know my clothes."

"Yeah, he does okay." There was a long silence, each concentrating on the meal.

Gus came back, sat down and started eating again.

"Gus, George here was asking me again what you do for a living."
George tried vainly to wave Tony to silence, but failed.
"He a good friend?" Gus asked, not looking up.
"The best, I trust him like family."
"It's all right, Tony, let it drop," George said quietly, glancing nervously at Gus.

Gus pushed his plate away and wiped his mouth and chin on the large checkered napkin. "Go ahead and tell him, if it means so damn much."

Tony motioned George to lean closer. "Now this is strictly because of us bein' friends, George. Gus here gets paid for removin' unwanteds, if you get my drift."

"Jesus H. Christ, Tony. I'm not sure I wanted to know that!"

Gus said nothing, a thin smile on his face, picking his teeth with a large silver pick he had fetched from his vest pocket.

George's curiosity overcame caution. "Gus, just suppose someone wanted me 'removed,' what would it cost them?"

Gus sat up. The smile left his face, his eyes now cold and calculating. He looked at George as one looks at a side of beef in a locker.

"You anybody?" Gus asked in a flat tone.

"What? Oh, you mean important? Maybe in this little town way out in Washington, Washington State, that is. No, I have to say in all honesty, I'm basically your run-of-the-mill nobody."

Gus looked him up and down once more. "Oh, a hundred, maybe a hundred and a half would buy it."

George's mouth dropped open. He said nothing.

Gus got up, extending his hand to George. "It was nice to meet you, Mister Stern. I hope you have a safe trip home." His face broke out in a wide grin. "Keep a sharp lookout. There's some bad elements in this town." He ambled to the door and out.

"You've had me, you sonnavabitch," George said to Tony.

"No, George, on my mother's soul, it's true." Tony threw some money on the table and headed for the door, George following in his wake.

Later, in the cab on his way back to the hotel, George shook his head and mumbled, "A hundred fifty dollars!"

"You say something, sir?" the cabby asked.

"No. Sorry. Just thinking about the price of beef."

During dinner that evening, after attending the play, George told Anna that because of a telephone call he had made earlier to the bank in Aurora, it would be necessary to cut his trip short and return home. "New regulations, just announced by the government, makes it critical I be at the bank as soon as possible. I want you to stay on. You have money to carry you awhile and an opportunity to see this dream of yours through. Will you do that for me?"

"You're right, a few more days won't hurt. Thanks for being so understanding." Anna smiled at him.

George paused, taking a sip of water, then leaned back against the tufted material of their booth. "Charlie said something to me today that sounded an alarm in my head, made me pause and reflect. He said, 'You're the bank.'" George spread his hands in a jester of mild frustration. "I'm not the bank. I'm not the 'cold storage.' It's nice to be called 'Mister' and 'Sir' and get special attention, I won't deny I don't enjoy, even abuse, it at times." George chuckled, embarrassed. "But I want people to see that I own a shirt with a frayed collar and a pair of boots with mud on them. I want people to smell me, know I don't bathe every hour on the hour. I want ladies to talk about seeing me with dirt under my nails or my shirttail hanging out. Am I making any sense?"

"Yes," Anna said quietly, reassuringly.

"I don't mean I want to get drunk in public or fart in church."

Anna laughed. "You did when you were young, why not now?"

"I guess I want people to know me as me!"

"George, you're respected for your integrity, your genuineness, your concern for others, your near obsession with honesty and fair dealings. People look up to you because you deserve and earned all these things. People may be ignorant, but most are not dumb. You have a lasting quality that endures and strengthens with time. You are a leader, George—dirty nails or no. You lead, not because you choose to, but because others choose to follow."

"Well, flattery will get you anything, my dear." He tried to make light of her comments, but he was deeply moved. It was nearing midnight. "Come on, Anna, it's almost the witching hour. Tomorrow may be a Cinderella day for you." He paid the waiter and helped Anna with her wrap.

Riding back to the hotel, George put his hand on Anna's arm, "Good time tonight?"

"The best." She leaned her head on his shoulder.

They rode the rest of the way in silence.

Chapter 16

Despite her best efforts, Anna was unsuccessful in attracting an agent's genuine interest in her book. One seemed interested, and Anna's spirits lifted, until over lunch he suggested a roll in the hay might best pay his commission a few days a week.

"We definitely have a misunderstanding." Anna had said, snatched her manuscript from the table, and in the process purposely spilled her glass of port wine on his shirt and trousers.

Unfortunately, her morning's efforts proved fruitless. It was nearing noon as she entered an older, well-maintained office building on Broadway, close by Herald Square. She searched the registry in the lobby, noting the office of Northshield and Associates, Publishing Agents, Room 523. Departing the elevator, she hurried to the office only to find the door locked and the lights out. As she turned to leave, a door closed down the hall and a man strolled toward her, drying his hands on a towel. "May I help you, Miss?" he asked pleasantly, walking to room 523 and unlocking the door.

"Mister Northshield?"

"Yes?" He paused in the doorway.

"I was coming to see you, or at least someone in your office."

"Are you responding to the secretarial position? I'm sorry; we filled that this morning." He went inside, leaving the door ajar.

Anna walked back to the office, her footsteps echoing in the empty hallway. She pushed the door open. "I'm not looking for a job, I'm looking for an agent."

He reentered the small office area. "Sorry, I just presumed...."

"That because I am a woman I must be a secretary?" she interrupted.

He grinned. "Actually, I was going to say I presumed because you are so pretty and well turned out, you would most likely be a secretary."

"If they're pretty, they can't have brains, is that what you're saying, Mister Northshield?"

He put up his hands in mock protection and walked toward her. "Steven J. Northshield, Miss, at your service."

"My name is Anna Stern, Mister Northshield." She extended her hand. "I'm an author looking for an agent. I'm sorry for my little outburst, this has not been one of my better days."

"Perhaps we should start over. Have you had lunch? I was just on my way and would be happy to have you join me. We could talk about your manuscript."

Anna thought about the recent luncheon with another agent and its outcome, but reconsidered. "I'd be delighted."

A telephone jangled in an inside office. "Sorry, my phone. You can wait in my office if you wish."

She went inside. The office was larger than she had imagined, judging by the small outer office area. Northshield's desk was of rich oak grain; his high-backed chair upholstered in rich leather, including the arm rests. On one wall a built-in bookcase of matching oak covered the entire wall, the shelves filled with books, manuscripts, mementos, and two carvings, one of which especially attracted Anna. A bust of a woman, honed from black mahogany, apparently simulating an African or perhaps Asian tribe, the face featured broad nose and nostrils, arched brow, the upper lip slightly protruding over the lower. There was evidence of bands or rings about the neck, hair pulled tightly back against the handsome head.

Immediately behind Northshield's chair was a credenza also laden with manuscripts—and a photograph of his wife and two small children smiling directly into the camera. Anna studied the woman's face and liked her immediately. Two more chairs matched the comfortable leather chair Anna selected. The wall opposite the bookcases contained watercolor seascapes and a draped window facing the street. The carpet was rich beige, of quality wool. Anna presumed, correctly, that Northshield and Associates was reasonably successful. Anna watched Northshield as he spoke in a pleasant, modulated voice. He was nearly six feet tall but looked taller because of his slender frame; his face was pleasant with smile lines in his cheeks, crinkle lines near his grey-green eyes. He obviously enjoyed life. Anna thought him a most handsome man.

"Do you live in New York?" Northshield asked as they waited in the restaurant lounge to be seated.

"No, Washington."

"Beautiful city. Love the historical flavor."

"I should learn after a while," Anna interrupted. "The state of Washington, small town named Aurora."

"What brings you all the way to New York?"

"My brother raises and markets apples. He travels east twice each year, and I had an opportunity to come with him. Unfortunately he had to leave this morning, his bank is under a bit of pressure so he felt it important to return."

"He must be busy... fruit broker, banker..."

"He stays involved," she smiled.

"Tell me about your manuscript, Miss Stern."

"It's a rather simple story, really. A small girl in Germany growing up in the late eighteen hundreds and her dream of freedom in America. Her hopes and desires rise and fall, as do those of the builders and promoters of the Statue of Liberty, or 'The Mother of Exiles,' as Emma Lazarus called her in her beautiful poem. I want to see her again, as I saw her when my family and I arrived here nearly twenty-six years ago by ship. I've carried that moment in my heart ever since." She felt a sudden surge, a desire to cry, but quickly gained control of her emotions. "Anyway," Anna continued, "my manuscript ties the struggle of one individual—the young German girl—to gain her opportunity to come to America with the bigger, historical struggle and hardships to bring the statue to America. I'd call my book fiction, laced with strong historical facts."

He smiled at her, their eyes holding for a moment.

Anna looked away, a slight flush coloring her face. Her attraction to this man she had met less than an hour ago was too strong. She comforted herself knowing he was married, which provided the perfect out should circumstances require a quick and legitimate termination.

They ate slowly. Anna told him of her failed book agent experiences to date. He explained how his father had started the business and that he, Steven, having graduated from New York University in journalism with a minor in dramatic arts, had drifted into the business after trying his hand as a cub reporter on the *New York Times*. "I'm the 'Associate' part of the firm's name."

Lunch completed, they returned to his office to review the manuscript in earnest.

He read the first few lines, nodding. He moved ahead several pages, stopped and read quickly, scanning the words. He continued reviewing, pausing occasionally to make notations on a pad on his desk. After ten minutes he put the manuscript aside. "It has possibilities. You seem to work the historical information in without burdening the story." He reviewed his notes. "Dialogue is a little weak, but not bad, just needs some polishing. Typical of most first manuscripts. A little editing or rewriting should solve that."

"Then you'll represent me!" Anna said, overjoyed.

"I didn't say that, Anna. It has possibilities." Steven came around the desk and leaned against it. "Would you be willing to do something for me—for you, actually—that may make this a marketable item?"

"Yes, of course."

"I have a friend who was an editor in a small publishing house until it went out of business a couple years back. He does freelancing for several firms in town. What he will do, for a fee, is review your manuscript more carefully than I and suggest changes, collaborate with you in making the changes, or do them himself, and then have you approve them. Sound interesting?"

"You said a fee?"

"Reasonable rate—usually by the hour. You could accomplish a lot for, say, a hundred dollars." No guarantees, of course."

"Of course," Anna said. She liked Steven very much and felt she could trust him. "Would you take the time—now, hopefully—to go over a page or two and show me what he would do?" She wanted to maintain a contact with him. If he sent her to his friend, her chances seemed more remote.

"Yes, but I can't right now." He looked at his watch. "I have a film director coming by in a few minutes, and we need to review some contracts. I'll be held up the rest of the afternoon. I'm sorry."

"I'm disappointed, too." Anna tried not to let her words reveal the depth of her unhappiness. *You must remember he is married,* she reprimanded herself. She looked at the picture of his wife and envied her good fortune.

"I am sorry, Anna. I hope you understand and you'll think about my suggestion and get back to me?" Steven asked.

"Yes. Thank you for the wonderful lunch, and your time. It's been a great pleasure meeting you."

"Anna, I could come by your hotel after work if that would help."

"Your wife may not approve, Mister Northshield," Anna said, a touch of anger in her voice. Maybe she had misjudged him; he was just a little smoother than the others.

"My wife?"

"Now, now, Mister Northshield, certainly you haven't forgotten her and your two beautiful youngsters."

"Anna! Wait! I'm not married."

"The portrait on your desk; Barbara on the telephone!"

Steven started laughing, the sound rising to a great crescendo. "The picture is of my sister Barbara and her kids."

Anna felt like a fool, a fool of her own making. "You have my address," she said in a businesslike tone. "I'll expect you at seven."

Chapter 17

The ringing of the telephone startled Anna. She glanced at her watch; it said 7:15.pm.

"Yes?"

"A gentleman to see you, Miss Stern," the desk clerk said. "A Steven Northshield."

"Thank you. Tell him to come up, please. I've been expecting him."

Upon leaving Steven's office, Anna had hailed a cab and rushed back to her hotel. As the taxi wended its way through the afternoon congestion, she tried to bring her emotions and thoughts under control. Her ability to be calm and passive during periods of emotional strife had always been a point of personal pride. In the main, and especially when it concerned a hint of romantic involvement, she was able to push her feelings aside and cool her ardor, and therefore that of a suitor. This time was different. She was anxious to see Steven again, to talk with him, to perhaps touch or be touched by him.

As seven o'clock had approached, Anna became frustrated. One moment she cursed herself for being so bold and thought of calling and cancelling. The next moment, the time could not pass quickly enough. What would she say? What would they talk about? She tried recalling his features and his voice, already becoming blurred in her memory. One moment she was foolish, giddy; the next minute frightened, then elated, then sick to her stomach, then walking on air.

The warm shower she had hoped would calm her seemed instead to enhance the longings, a desire for him. Exiting the shower, she had studied herself in the mirrored wall as if seeing her reflection for the first time. The awareness of her splendid figure had not gone unnoticed by Anna—and certainly not by men. She was aware of their stares, the sometime crude endeavors to gain her favor. She considered her body a cURSe of sorts; an impediment to acceptance by other women, the failure to be considered an intellectual equal by men.

She prepared carefully. Her hair clean and shiny, a drop of elegant perfume subtly placed on nape of neck, crook of elbows, behind her knees and the cleavage between her breasts, cosmetics meticulously applied. For her dress she chose a simple blue silk frock with modest scooped neckline, gathered at her trim waist then flaring over her ample hips, sheer silk stockings; matching pale blue pumps completed the ensemble.

As she went to answer the muted tapping on the door, she hesitated a moment in front of the entrance hall mirror to examine her hair, then opened the door.

"You're late."

"Miss Stern?"

"Yes."

A handsome, well-dressed gentleman stood in the doorway.

"I'm Steven Northshield Senior, Steve's father. May I come in a moment?"

Anna was stunned, her surprise apparent. "Why, yes, by all means."

"Steve didn't want to leave a cold little message with the desk clerk so asked that I come by personally and extend his regrets. He also wanted you to have the name of the freelance editor; you'll find his name and number inside this envelope and a manuscript. He suggested you read it at your leisure. It contains the original text and a revised text of a very successful book we recently had the good fortune to represent. Steve hopes it might provide some insight into what you and the freelance editor might accomplish with your story."

"It was very thoughtful of you to go out of your way for me. Did Steven say when he might call?"

"No. He's in Boston completing contract negotiations for movie rights to a recently published book. It may be several days. I am sorry, I really must run. Good night, Miss Stern."

Anna watched him to the elevator and waved, then closed the door. As she leaned against the inside jamb, tears came quickly. The week had been wearing on her both physically and mentally. Some good had perhaps come of it: an agent was interested enough in her manuscript to help her, but she wondered if she would see him again. She ordered a light dinner through room service, then rolled the serving cart into the hall and threw home the night lock on the door, exposing the 'Do Not Disturb' message. It was dark when she pulled the drapes and turned off the radio.

With the manuscript in hand she entered the bedroom, disrobed, and climbed into bed. She reviewed the writings carefully, noting the impact the choice of a word or a rearranged sentence could have on holding a reader's attention, conveying the author's intent. Time passed quickly and she grew sleepy. She turned out the light and fell into a troubled sleep, the disappointment of the evening still weighing on her mind. Early in the morning hours, Anna was startled awake by the dampness of her perspiration against the linens. For years, she had periodically dreamed of seeing her mother floating face-down in the river. She would wade to the body and turn it over, not wanting to turn it over for she would see not her mother's face, but her own.

Now, as in the past, Anna considered this an ominous portent of her pending insanity. She rose and went to the bathroom, ran cool water across her wrists and arms, sponged her face, neck, and torso with a dampened washcloth. She started to cry, standing on the coldness of the tile, seeing herself reflected in the mirror. A beautiful woman, who would not, could not, impose her mother's curse on any man. *How I hate you, Mother, for what you've done to me.* She broke into uncontrollable sobs, her body weak with the strain of the nightmare. She returned to the bed and was soon asleep—this time the deep, undisturbed sleep of exhaustion.

Anna awoke late Saturday morning. Lying in bed, she recalled her nightmare and determination to avoid seeing Steven again. The manuscript he had sent would be wrapped and mailed back, a polite note of thanks enclosed and saying good-bye. She would forgo her dreams of becoming a writer and return to Aurora. Teaching was rewarding. She was confident she could find a job somewhere; if not, she would live with George and Sarah, waiting for her insanity to come and put her tortured mind to rest. Tears again welled in her eyes, and she let them flow, not caring.

She brushed her teeth and ran a comb indifferently through her hair. Despite the long sleep, her eyes were red and swollen with dark circles showing beneath them.

She suddenly remembered the night lock; the maid wouldn't be able get in to change the sweat-stained sheets. Slipping into her robe, she hurried to unlatch the door, opening the draperies as she went, letting the sunshine flood the room. As she neared the door, she heard a light tapping and hurried to open it for the maid.

Chapter 18

"Hello, Anna Stern. I hope these flowers will partly make up for last night," Steven said, a friendly, happy smile on his face. He held a bouquet of bright chrysanthemums and daisies.

Anna's surprise turned quickly to embarrassment as she remembered her unkempt appearance, her nakedness—save for thin panties beneath the robe she had so casually donned. Self-consciously she pulled the robe tightly around her. Her first thought was to turn and flee, to take refuge in the bedroom.

"I should have called first, but I wanted to see you, to surprise you." He was embarrassed for his action, his tone evidencing his concern.

"You succeeded on both counts," she said, an edge in her voice. "Well, don't stand out in the hall, come in."

"Anna, I don't know what to say...." His expression told her he noticed her eyes, red, swollen, full of pain. "I completed the contract negotiations early this morning, so I drove back from Boston, managed three hours' sleep and a shower at my apartment, then hurried over, hoping against hope you were in your rooms. You've been crying. Is something wrong? Is it your brother or your family?"

Anna shook her head. *God, why did he come? What am I going to do?* she thought, trying to clear her head to make sense of this somewhat bizarre turn of events. "It's nothing, really, nothing for you to worry about. I'll be all right. Would you like to sit down? I'm afraid the place is a bit of a mess. I just got up, and the maid hasn't been by."

He walked to one of the davenports near the fireplace and sat down, flowers still in his hand. "Uh, do you have some place for these?" He extended the bouquet toward her.

"I'll see if I can find a vase."

She knelt down, looking on the lower shelves of the bookcase, careful to secure the upper portion of her robe with one hand, but allowing a substantial portion of her legs to become exposed, not unnoticed by Steve. Embarrassed, she attempted to pull the garment over her legs, teetered backward and sprawled onto her back. The robe, now loosened, flew open, fully exposing her legs, her silk panties providing the minimum of modesty. Momentarily stunned, it was seconds before she had presence of mind to regain her composure and cover herself. "Goddamn it!" she blurted out.

He was beside her now, kneeling, the flowers thrown onto the coffee table.

"Are you hurt, Anna? Are you all right?"

"I'm fine. Just my pride and my dignity, and maybe a bruised... cheek." She rubbed her backside where she had hit the corner of the raised hearth.

"Let me help you up." He reached for her hands.

"No. I can manage quite nicely by myself," she said, her voice carrying a strong note of indignation. "You can find your own vase!" Rolling onto her side away from him, she managed to rise to her feet without further incident.

Steven returned to the davenport and slumped into the cushions, his posture and face showing signs of dejection. He sat staring at the carpet, tracing a seam line back and forth with the edge of his shoe. She came to the back of the davenport across from him and stood looking at him, her head tilted slightly to one side.

"Do you really want to do something nice for me?" she asked.

"Get up and go home?" he answered.

Her voice easier now, the anger gone, "Call down and order breakfast while I take a shower. Tell them I'll need fresh linens as well as fresh towels."

"Sure, I think I can handle that," Steve said, his voice sounding more cheery.

As she stood in the shower, she knew she could not resist being with him, despite the promise to herself less than an hour ago. She wondered what it would be like making love with him. Still a virgin, she could only imagine. She smiled, pondering if his hands would be as hot and stimulating as the shower spray. A warmth she had never experienced coursed through her body, making her legs unsteady. She was surprised to see her nipples rise, her breasts fuller.

In the living room, Steven had let the maid in, then out as she quickly and expertly changed the bed and placed fresh towels just outside the bathroom door. The waiter came with Anna's breakfast and left.

Steven worried that Anna was all right; it had been several minutes since the shower was turned on. He visualized her naked in the shower, remembering the glimpse of her nearly exposed breasts, her long, supple legs, the shadowy triangle through her filmy panties. The thoughts of her—close, wet, and sweet-smelling—made his member swell against the restraint of his shorts.

Anna turned off the water. The extended shower had filled the room with steam, the humidity uncomfortable. She pushed open the bathroom door and the steam rushed past her into the bedroom. She noticed the freshly made bed and the towels beside the door. She retrieved one.

"I thought maybe you'd washed away, I was getting concerned," Steve's voice came from the next room. "Food's here, don't want it to get cold."

"I'm drying off. I'll be right out. Have some coffee while you're waiting."

"I did, and it's delicious. Want me to bring you a cup?" His voice was jovial yet had an undertone of pleading.

"Yes, please." Anna was frightened by her boldness so stepped back into the safety of the bathroom.

He came in glancing about, the cup rattling noticeably in its saucer. The steam—and therefore her protection—had vanished. He peered through the last remnants of vapor and saw her standing against the bathroom wall, a towel held delicately in front of her.

"Your coffee. I'll just set it down here." His eyes never left hers as he moved to the near side of the bed, placing the cup and saucer on the bedside table. They were less than five feet apart now, each one's desire at fever pitch.

"Are you going to stay in there all day?" His voice was low, urging.

"I may...need a little help."

He threw off his jacket and tie, then moved toward her slowly. She could see the need in his eyes. He was closer, now against her. The towel floated to the floor between them. Their lips touched, soft, warm, yielding to each other. Her still wet body was pressed against him, dampening his shirt and pants, outlining his manliness in stark detail.

"Anna, oh, Anna," he whispered into her ear. "I know this sounds foolish, but I love you. God, do I love you!"

"Oh, my dearest," she whispered back.

His fingers caressed her back and buttocks, then moved to her face, cradling it tenderly, kissing her nose, eyes, and lips. Her modesty had left. She knew she wanted him and for him to have her. Without speaking they moved to the bed, she folding back the comforter as he undressed. Steven was more muscular than she had thought, his stomach flat with washboard-like ridges running from his sternum to navel. Legs, straight and lean, lightly coated with hair to match that of his arms. A heavier, thicker mat spread across his chest and the area just above his fully extended member. He came to her, pulling her firmly to him, her breasts flattened against his torso. His erection, hard and demanding, pushed upward between them as they stood straining to touch, flesh on flesh.

"Come lie down, darling," he urged.

She obeyed, her body fully exposed, long legs extended; large, now-heaving breasts falling away to the softness of her slender waist. She watched as Steve's eyes traveled down, down to her pubic hair, still wet from the shower, her legs still shiny with dampness. He moved onto the bed beside her, caressing her shoulder with his lips, moving softly to the deep valley between her breasts, cupping one and then the other to kiss each nipple with mouth and tongue.

She was nearly out of control wanting desperately to participate. Suddenly, clearly, she remembered a discussion with Sarah as they talked of Anna's virginity and the possibility of her first sexual encounter. "Let the pleasure come naturally. Don't be afraid to be touched or to touch. Be a little bold," Sarah had told her. His hand slid along her side, caressing and touching her as he moved. "You're magic, my darling," he moaned, kissing her stomach.

She raised her hips, rotating them against his face as he grew bolder with mouth and tongue, smelling and tasting her wetness, the opening pink and tight to his pressure. He paused, "Darling, I must ask you, and you must tell me. Are you a virgin?"

"Oh, Steve, is it that obvious?"

"No, my darling, no. But now that I know, I'll be even more gentle."

"Oh, Steve, just hold me...and help me...I want you...soon!"

"We're nearly there, my dearest."

He touched her again, caressing, moving his fingers, seeking and finding. She let out a sharp cry of joy, her wetness signaling her readiness.

"Now, darling, now," he said in a low, demanding voice. "Move with me, work with me." He entered her slowly, almost teasingly, spreading the previously untouched channel.

"In!" she begged. "In!" She moved against him, moving now to his motion as he had asked.

She cried out.

"Oh, Anna, darling, did I hurt you?"

"No! No! Don't stop." Her head was rolling from side to side, her hips and buttocks meeting his increasing strokes. A wave of total pleasure surged within her body, then again and yet again. She could not believe the wonder of the moment.

"Oh, sweet Anna!" Steve cried out, matching her pleasure with his own.

She started to speak, then felt him burst inside her as she again experienced surge after surge of joy. He sank gently down upon her, kissing her face, her lips, burying his face in her hair, softly touching her breasts. He rolled to one side, bringing her with him, his hands now gentle on her back and soft buttocks. She responded with small kisses, touching his chest and stomach.

He rolled onto his back, she still on her side, looking at him, marveling at what had just occurred. Exhausted, she lay back, their hands seeking, then joining together.

"Anna."

"Yes, darling?"

"You have a hell of a bruise on your butt."

They rolled together, laughing, embracing, finally falling asleep in each other's arms, Anna's nightmare washed away by the security she knew she had found.

George had been home three days. It was evening, and Sarah and Gina were putting the last of the clean supper dishes in the cupboard when the doorbell rang and he went to answer it. He entered the kitchen, a telegram clutched in his hand. Slitting the yellow envelope open, he scanned the words, then read them again more carefully. "I'll be go to hell," he said in an astonished voice.

"What?" Sarah asked.

"'MANUSCRIPT ACCEPTED. STOP.

"LIFE WONDERFUL. STOP.

"MARRIAGE CURES ALL. STOP.

"YOU'LL LOVE HIM. STOP.'

"It's signed Mrs. Steven Stern Northshield."

Chapter 19

George sat in the living room of the Homeplace. He gazed across the barren orchard to the river beyond, watching the mist rise slowly as the late February sun warmed the water of the unhurried stream. Peaceful now, it would gather strength in the late spring runoff, swelling to a torrent, threatening to overpower the restraints imposed by the river channel's high banks.

The view was so embedded and familiar, as though time had segmented itself and thrown away forty years. Except for upgrading and modernization, the old two-story house retained the same charm and elegance it held at the turn of the century. Following Sarah's sudden death two years before, he sold Ridgemont and returned to the home he had always loved, his need of linkage to the past important as he grew older. Here he could remember the happiest times in his life, with Anna, Sarah and Gina. He, strong and active, working to produce the wonders of the harvest, the sense of pride and fulfillment that all his success at the warehouse, the bank, the new shopping center could not match.

Today was like so many days his beloved Sarah and he had sat looking out to the river and hills beyond, planning and dreaming of the future—a future now come and nearly gone. The cold outside matched the emptiness in his heart as he remembered his last day with Sarah.

"Don't be late, old woman. We dare not miss the Grand Opening!"

Still meticulous in appearance, Sarah had chosen a blue suit, one he had often complimented her on, and a flowered blouse with a soft bow at the neckline.

"You look beautiful." His words spoken as a caress.

"Thank you, kind sir, but I doubt a woman of sixty-eight is going to turn too many heads today."

He took her arm, and together they hurried out the back door to the car.

The concept of the shopping center was first born in George's mind following a trip to Los Angeles to visit Steve and Anna. A parcel of land he and Sarah had discussed so long ago then purchased shortly after the end of World War II was ideal for the center. Acting as a hub for the housing and commercial developments that occurred in the late forties and on through the fifties, the center was the crown jewel of the well-conceived and carried-out master plan of the Stern Subdivision, North. Several tenants had occupied Aurora Mall for some weeks, but the official opening of the twenty-eight stores was in held in April 1958.

As George and Sarah arrived, a small contingent of city and county officials, the mall manager, and two hundred or more members of the community gathered. A smattering of applause welcomed their arrival.

"Ladies and gentlemen." The mayor was on a raised platform situated directly in front of the main mall entrance. "I usually like to make long-winded speeches..."

The audience laughed politely.

"...But today belongs to the man and his lovely wife, who envisioned this marvelous addition to our fair community. The benefits of bringing the citizenry from outlying towns and villages enhances all of us and increases Aurora's position as the center, the hub, of this vast and wealthy valley. It is men like George Stern with the foresight, the desire, and the resources, who can make a dream of this magnitude come to full bloom. I'm proud, I'm honored, to present my friend—and yours—George Stern!"

George stepped to the platform, aiding Sarah with a steadying hand. He remembered a platform similar to this when he reassured a frightened town with promises of providing them a bank and a secure future. As then, he held up his arms, requesting quiet.

"Thank you, Mister Mayor," he glanced about, "other guests,

ladies, gentlemen." He cleared his throat. "This is a dream my wife Sarah and I have had for almost forty years. No, we didn't imagine a shopping center forty years ago, but we did imagine a future for Aurora, our home. We hope you enjoy and use this center. To us it represents a symbol of the strength and tenacity of the people of this valley to survive and prosper and grow. In many ways it is the fruit of Sarah's and my life. The bringing in of the last load, if you will, of our years of work and planning. Thanks to many of you and your parents before you, we reap the harvest of all our efforts. Thank you for your kind attention. Now go, enjoy!"

The crowd responded with a quick burst of sincere applause, a few shouts, then moved away quickly. After another round of hand-shaking and polite words of thanks and praise to and from the dignitaries, George and Sarah strolled through the mall, stopping to talk with friends, examining store displays—a happy, relaxing afternoon. They bought ice creams, and like two children, ordered sprinkles. Shortly after four they entered their car and returned to Ridgemont.

The sun was setting as they entered the house. Sarah moved about, turning on lights against the pending dusk. "What would you like for dinner?" she asked.

"Let's not end the celebration now. How about dinner out—kind of top off the day?"

"Wonderful idea." She reached up and kissed him.

She moved to the stairway. "Think I'll put my head down a few minutes. Come wake me in an hour or so?"

He pecked her on the cheek. "Have a good rest. Sweet dreams."

He watched her climb the stairs. She turned at the top landing and smiled at him, blowing him a kiss. "I'll save this for later," he said, putting the kiss in his inside coat pocket. She turned, and he heard the bedroom door close behind her.

Time passed; darkness was total now. George moved about the room, pulling the heavy drapes against the coolness of the early spring evening, then went upstairs. Sarah lay on their bed, a small night lamp providing a soft glow in the room. A warm blanket covered her body, drawn up against her face. He looked at her, peaceful and serene, then sat beside her on the bed.

"Hey, sleepyhead, time to get up." He shook her shoulder gently.

Her arm slid slowly from its resting place on her hip and lay motionless, hand turned outward.

"Sarah?"

She did not move. Quickly he rolled her onto her back, threw the blanket aside, seeking the sound of a heartbeat against her chest. He met only silence. He sank beside her, not believing what he knew was true.

"You promised you wouldn't leave me, old woman, you promised," he sobbed, the big, empty house the only witness to his heartbreak.

Sarah was buried the following Wednesday with simple graveside services. As was her wish, her cremated remains were place in an urn and buried beside her father in the family plot. There was no open casket, Sarah believing the last remembrances of a departed should be that of a living, active being, not of artificial repose. Anna and Steve Northshield flew from Los Angeles to attend. The services ended before noon. George, Anna, Steve, Gina, and Flynn, Gina's husband, returned home, now suddenly quiet and hushed after the onslaught of the last few days.

The strain of the ordeal was apparent on their faces as they filed into the large living room and found a chair or davenport on which to rest—each lost in his or her memories of Sarah, recalling moments from the recesses of the mind, wanting to share, yet jealously guarded as a rare and valued treasure, knowing once exposed to the examination of others, its uniqueness would be forever lost. More time passed, bodies relaxing, minds allowed to drift and revitalize. George broke the silence. "When did you say you were moving to Hawaii, Anna?"

"We hope this fall if we can wrap up our business affairs."

"I need to return home to get those business affairs completed," Steve said. "As for Anna?"

"I'll stay as long as I'm needed." She rose and walked to her brother's side.

Anna's extended visit made George's slow transition to a new life without Sarah more bearable. For her part, Anna enjoyed the quietness and measured pace of Aurora. "It's as if I'd never been away," she said to George as they sat sipping an after-dinner cordial in the familiar surroundings of his library. "As you know, Steve is anxious to move to the Islands. My visit has convinced me what this old body needs is fresh air and solitude. It's time I went home and get ready to move."

He came to her, and they embraced.

"Thank you for being here for me, Wee One," he whispered.

Chapter 20

Ted Jaffey rolled over in his king-sized bed and squinted at his bedside clock, nearly eleven. No hurry, his handball match was at two-thirty, and Saturdays meant the court would not be free until closer to three. He stretched his lean, tanned body to its fullest, his toes and fingers spread and extended as a cat upon waking from a nap on a sun-drenched carpet. He was fifty-one but looked forty-one; the only betrayal of time was his silver-white hair and a slight sag of skin beneath his jaw.

He had joined the rapidly expanding Freeland Bank in 1951 as a loan officer, having graduated from college in 1949 with a degree in Business and Economics, using his G.I. Bill, some money his Aunt Rachel had bequeathed him, and a football scholarship. Always an excellent athlete, he was drafted by the Chicago Bears but failed to make the roster after suffering a debilitating hamstring pull.

He lay contemplating the changes in the hierarchy of Freeland once Charlie Wesslin retired in the fall. His obvious rivals for the position of president were Ed Gilbert, Senior Cashier and Corporate Treasurer; Tony Welch, Vice President, Deposit Division; Flynn Donovan, Vice President, Commercial Loans. Of the three, he considered Flynn his most formidable opponent, even though he was Flynn's boss. First, Flynn was George Stern's son-in-law, and thus carried the support of the bank's board chairman and major stockholder; secondly, the staff and the community admired Flynn, powerful attributes in Stern's business philosophy.

He rose and entered the adjoining weight room to perform his daily thirty-minute exercise ritual, his thoughts now focused on his upcoming week's vacation in Las Vegas.

REAP THE HARVEST

*

It seemed sheer luck that Ted found a poker game and at stakes he felt he could afford. While sitting in the lounge, he became engaged in conversation with two men sitting in an adjoining booth. They exchanged pleasantries, sharing brief personal histories as one often does upon meeting strangers. Later Bill Hartley had sought him out and asked him to join them as a fourth in a poker game. The $5000.00 required to sit in bothered Ted initially, but he considered himself a good poker player and he had the funds available.

The other players were in the suite when he arrived. Bill Hartley and Byrum Barnes, whom he had met earlier, introduced to the forth player, Douglas Young of Hawaii. In contrast to the bulky size of Hartley and Barnes, Young was of slight build, with small, almost delicate hands. His dark, piercing eyes belied the impression of a man of weakness, giving an air of conceit, Ted thought, yet more likened perhaps to an inscrutable Oriental. As the evening wore on, Ted determined his initial evaluation of Young most accurate. They played for three hours, the bets gradually growing in size, the pots occasionally containing several thousand dollars. Ted managed to hold his own and accumulate an additional eight thousand dollars; however, a major pot eluded him.

"I'm hungry," Hartley said. "Let's break and order up some food. I'll see if we can find a hostess to hustle our food and drinks." Minutes later a cart containing sliced meats, cheeses, breads and various relishes was pushed into the room. The lower shelf held liquors, mixers, a bucket of ice and several glasses. Ted's attention was immediately drawn to the young hostess. Oriental, perhaps Eurasian; olive-skinned; dark, wide-set eyes; jet-black hair pulled tight against her head, then gathered by a large golden comb in back. Her uniform was tasteful: a mandarin collar with an open neckline, exposing a portion of her high, firm breasts. The slit sides of her skirt ran to just below the top of her hips, showing her trim, long legs.

"My name is Lisa." She bowed, her voice low, a slight lisping sound in her speech.

They ordered. Jaffey requested Canadian Mist and ice.

Lisa brought their drinks, then sat across the room on a small chair near the window, her position in direct line of sight whenever Ted looked up. Her dress had fallen away from her legs, revealing their exquisite beauty. Occasionally their eyes met, and she smiled politely. The afternoon wore on to mid-evening. Lisa continued to be the perfect hostess—beautiful, quiet, and efficient. On at least two occasions, Lisa pressed against Ted's shoulder with her hip or turned to brush her lower stomach against him, as if by chance but his effort to read her face or smile was fruitless.

"Mister Jaffey, it's your bet," Young said.

"How much to me?" Ted asked.

"Ten thousand."

Ted rechecked his hole card, the queen of hearts, plus the two queens up gave him three of a kind, the fourth card the nine of diamonds.

Hartley had a pair of sevens and a ten, maybe two pair, depending on his hole card; Barnes had folded and was sipping his drink, watching the action. Young, two kings and the eight of clubs showing—possible three of a kind or two pair. In any event, it beat Hartley.

Ted's queens beat Young's two kings unless he had a king down. It all hinged on this last card. The game had been good to him and he could cover. "Ten thousand it is." Ted pushed the money forward, noting he would have only seven thousand left.

"I fold," said Hartley.

Ted was dealt the nine of clubs—full house—Young an eight of diamonds. Two pair showing, maybe a full house if he had a king or eight in the hole.

"Kings high bets."

"Twenty thousand," said Young.

Ted glanced at Lisa, who returned his look with a warm smile. She arched her back slightly, then ran her hand up her exposed leg, her eyes looking at him bright with promises.

"I'm light, I've only got seven grand in my kick"

"You're good for it, I'm sure, Mister Jaffey. I'll take your marker."

A thirteen thousand dollar marker! No, I can't, Ted thought, squirming in his seat. *But if I make this, I'll have a bundle. Young must have the three kings or he wouldn't bet so much. But, if he's bluffing...*

"Well, Mister Jaffey, do you feel lucky or is this one mine? Twenty thousand to you, sir."

"I call—damn right I call!" Ted said, pushing his money forward. "What have you got?"

"One moment, Mister Jaffey, the matter of your marker. Miss Lisa, paper and pen for Mister Jaffey, please."

Lisa walked across the room, smiling at Ted, her body swaying seductively. As she leaned over his shoulder he could smell her perfume, feel her breasts press against his shoulder.

"Is this all you desire, Mista Jaffey?" she asked, placing the pad and pen before him.

He looked up into her warm soft eyes, quickly wrote out the marker, signed it and tossed it in the middle of the table.

Young pulled his hole card, looking at it as if for the first time, tantalizingly, then placed it carefully face up—a king. Ted's face paled, his shoulders slumping.

"Too bad, Mister Jaffey, you lose. Now, when might I expect to be paid?"

"I'll have to make certain arrangements, but I'll pay you soon." Ted's mind reviewed his finances quickly; he did not have the money readily available.

"Lisa, pour Mister Jaffey another drink," Young said. He placed the ends of his fingertips together while studying Ted carefully. Ted gratefully swallowed the generous portion Lisa had provided. His head was hurting, the drinks suddenly taking their toll.

"Mister Jaffey. You appear to be an honest man, a man of integrity?"

"Yes."

"This marker could prove embarrassing to you. However, since we are both honorable men I will tear up this marker in exchange for another marker for twenty-five thousand dollars payable in two years. If you win, you can walk out with your marker and a nice bundle of cash. We will play one hand of high card draw. You come out a big winner if you pull the right card."

Ted looked about, his eyes and mind not focusing as he wished. He noted both Barnes and Hartley had left the table. Lisa now sat next to him, her hand resting casually on his thigh. He glanced at her as she leaned forward. "You can do it, Mista Jaffey." She lowered her voice almost to a whisper. "I like winners, Mista Jaffey." Her hand moved up his leg and stopped, her fingers gently stroking. He looked at her lovely face; she was nodding encouragement.

"High card?"

"Yes."

"Two years to pay?"

"Only if you don't win."

Lisa's body pressed gently against his arm, her fingers higher now, searching.

"Okay. Deal."

Young quickly opened a new deck, shuffled, and passing the deck to Ted to be cut. Somehow Ted's glass was filled again, and he threw the liquor back into his throat with one gulp. Lisa's hand had stopped now and was resting softly against the bulge in Ted's pants, her face only inches away, smiling encouragement.

Ted passed the deck back and watch as the cards were fanned.

"First a new marker, Mister Jaffey. I've taken the liberty of having Mister Barnes make it out for you. All you need to do is sign." Young's voice was reassuring, quiet.

"Here is pen, Mista Jaffey," Lisa offered.

Ted, scarcely bothering to read the paper, signed.

"Go ahead, Mister Jaffey, you have the honors."

He hesitated, then with an inner prayer pulled a card, a ten.

"Very good, Mister Jaffey," Young said.

As in a dream, Ted watched Young extend his hand, moving slowly, hovering, then reached and turned over a queen. "Would you like double or nothing," asked Young, maintaining his cool tone.

"No." Ted's voice showed total resignation to his plight. "No."

"Gentlemen, would you be so kind to help Mister Jaffey to his room? Lisa, you go along. Be sure Mister Jaffey is made comfortable. Will you do that for me, please?"

"Yes, Mista Young."

Together they managed to navigate the hallway to the elevator and down to Ted's room. Barnes fished the room key from his pocket, and the three helped him to the bed.

"I'll stay a few minutes," Lisa said to the two men.

"Sure, honey, we understand. We'll leave you two lovebirds alone."

"Here, baby, let me help you get undressed. Then we have some fun?" Lisa whispered.

"Too sleepy. Sleep. Wanta sleep."

Ted lay on the bed, his head whirling. He could feel his clothes being removed, then Lisa standing beside the bed, naked.

"Turn off the light," he mumbled.

"In just a minute, baby," Lisa said.

She lay beside him, caressing him, holding him, lying on him and rolling him onto her. Minutes later she slid quietly from the bed. As he drifted toward a drunken sleep Lisa was beside him again, playing with him, arousing him, her mouth doing exciting things to which he could barely respond. He tried to open his eyes to be a part of the lovemaking, but he was too tired and drunk. At last darkness descended. He reached for her, but she was gone. His head sank into the soft pillow and he slept.

Ted awoke, not knowing what time it was, or even what day. He tried to bring his mind to bear on the poker game, the girl, but the constant pounding within his temples prevented him from doing so. Slowly, he raised to a sitting position, legs dangling over the bedside, elbows on his knees, his hands holding his head. The foul taste in his mouth and the smell of the liquor seeping from his pores made his stomach retch, bringing a sour emulsion into his throat and mouth.

Retrieving his shorts, he slipped into them and walked unsteadily to the window, pushed the curtains aside, and peered out. A light rain was falling, streaking the accumulated dust on the pane. He cranked open the two side windows, allowing the cool rain-fresh air to fill the room, set the air conditioning controls on cool, the fan on high, feeling the fresh air moving about him. After he showered, a welcome relief to his weary, ill-smelling body, he dried himself and returned to the bedroom, its coolness a shock against his skin. He closed the windows and curtains and adjusted the fan and temperature controls to seventy degrees then noticed a small envelope on the carpet just inside the door. It contained a single sheet of white stationery bearing the hotel's name and address.

Dear Teddy,
You were wonderful last night. The best.
Love,
Lisa

"I'll be damned," he said out loud, "even when I'm bombed, the ol' boy can still performs." He telephoned the front desk and discovered it was Thursday. The last he remembered was going to Suite 1136 Tuesday afternoon! No way could he have slept through a whole day he pondered. But indeed he had, nearly twenty-seven hours. The shower and fresh air had done wonders. Changing into clean clothing, he called room service, ordering orange juice, ham, eggs, hash browns, and coffee; he was famished. Breakfast finished, he dialed the front desk and discovered Young, Hartley and Barnes had checked out two days earlier. While some of the events remained fuzzy, he knew he owed Young twenty-five thousand dollars and did not have that kind of money. What had begun as an exciting, leisurely vacation was turning into a disaster.

Chapter 21

George visited Ed Gilbert in his office at the bank. Gilbert was fifty-two years old, intelligent, always prepared with pertinent facts and information for administrative and Board meetings. He enjoyed an excellent reputation within the banking community and was recruited from time to time by major banks on the West Coast. He and his family felt comfortable in the small town atmosphere and took advantage of the myriad of outdoor activities afforded them in and around Aurora. With the Freeland Bank but five years, he had been hired specifically to manage its fiscal and accounting needs.

George had developed an excellent working relationship with Ed, and in all probability would support him as next president over Ted Jaffey or his own son-in-law, Flynn Donovan.

"I need to visit with you in confidence, Ed. With Charlie's retirement scheduled for the end of the year, I'd like to get your thoughts on the direction you see the bank going, perhaps who you believe might make a good successor."

Ed paused, contemplating the question and the impact his answers might have. "Charlie has accomplished much for Freeland over the years. I admire him for many of the bolder moves he made right after the war. As an example, the branching into nearby communities showed vision, the ability to anticipate a need and fill it."

"Based on that observation, would you continue the same theme?" George asked.

"Well," Ed said with a grin, "I tend to be a little more cautious—my accounting background perhaps. We must be careful not to tie ourselves to too many fixed assets or long-term real estate loans. I'd push a little harder for consolidation of our position, maybe investigate the advantages of sale, lease back of current branch office buildings, definitely on any future locations. My research indicates strong advantages may exist by using carefully structured leases. More importantly, our liquidity position would be enhanced."

Ed stood looking out the window. "You know, George, we've all lapsed into a comfort zone, so to speak. Near full employment, stable rates, low inflation, no war on the horizon; but the good times may change. We should begin moving back to short-term loans and investments."

"Do you consider crop and construction loans short or long term? Our bank is based on aiding the ranchers and helping the community," George said.

"New construction is fine to the stronger builders. As to crop loans, I would like to see our commitment contain an option to review the rate every ninety to one-hundred eighty days."

"Sounds good from the bank's point of view, but we'd certainly get major resistance from borrowers."

"I'm a realist, George, I understand. You asked what direction I thought the bank should take, and I'm being very candid with you."

George joined Ed at the window. "It's strange to look out and see the changes over the last fifty-odd years—yet many things have changed so little. Same streets, many of the same buildings, just updated, more homes and orchards across the river, of course. At one time I could identify everyone's ranch, call each by a first name and tell you the kind of apples they grew or where they worked. Even knew most of their kids, but not anymore." He turned to Ed. "You didn't give me your thoughts about Charlie's successor."

"Well, the obvious are Ted, Tony, maybe Flynn."

"And yourself?"

"That's not for me to say."

"Does that mean you're not interested?"

"Interested? Damn right I am. But I'm also a team player. It's more important we get the right person for the job and for the right reasons. My strength is operations and I work well within that environment."

"What about Ted?"

"As I view it, the philosophy of this bank since its inception was supported on the strong back of the loan division. Ted is in a critical position to make or break this organization."

"Let me put it this way, and I want a direct answer: would Ted Jaffey make a good president of Freeland?"

"I'll answer this way. Loans are Charlie's strongest suit, and as long as Ted is smart enough to see which way Charlie wants to take us, Ted doesn't have to think, he just has to react. I don't think Ted's had many original business ideas in his life. He claims credit for his staff's ideas when Charlie likes the concepts; but if the idea doesn't fly, Ted will say it was so and so's suggestion and 'I told him it wouldn't work.' Either way, he wins. It makes me mad to see Tony, Ted's staff—hell, me, for that matter—work so damn hard and Ted get so much credit for doing so much less. Bottom line, I think he would be a very poor choice." Ed sank back in his chair.

"Thank you your counsel. I trust your judgement and appreciate your candor. Keep swingin', Ed, you ain't struck out yet."

The two shook hands as George took his leave.

Chapter 22

The following afternoon George returned to the bank. A light sprinkle of first snow had started to cover the ground. He went upstairs and entered Ted Jaffey's office.

After their initial greetings, George spoke. "I'll not take up much of your time. With Charlie's retirement coming at the end of the year, I'd like to get your feeling about the direction the bank is going, who you think the next president should be."

Ted leaned back in his chair. "I think the bank's directions are well-defined, I see no need to change—unless you have some suggestions, of course."

"So you're satisfied with the status quo? Continue to branch, build offices, continue current loan policies?"

"If Charlie wants it that way," Ted said

"Aren't you concerned we may tie up too much liquidity in fixed assets? After all, lack of cash impacts on the loan side more than anywhere else."

"You're right, perhaps a reevaluate is needed. Of course that's not really my area. Ed's our bookkeeper."

Calling Ed Gilbert a bookkeeper, not the accountant, did not escape George's notice.

"Be candid, Ted. If you had to make the decision regarding liquidity, what would you do? Forget Charlie for the moment, I'm asking you to make the decision. Assume you're our president for the moment."

"You said you thought we should stay more liquid, right?"

"No, I only posed the question."

"I'd say we generate liquidity," Ted sighed.

Ass-kisser, George said to himself. "One more question. How about yourself to succeed Charlie? You've been with us ten years, you know the ropes by now."

"Honest answer?"

"Yes, and confidential. It needn't leave this room," George assured him.

"I'm not always a modest man. I believe I'm the best choice."

"What about Tony or Ed, or someone else, say Flynn?"

"With all due respect to your son-in-law, he has a long way to go. He's not management material. Too friendly with the staff, doesn't set himself apart. Subordinates have to know who is boss; they have to respect your position, know you have the power."

"Tony? Ed?"

"Both great. Work very well with them. They see eye to eye with me on most everything. But Tony is strictly checking and savings—no loan experience—and Ed, well, if the bookkeepers had it their way, I like Ed and respect him, but his job is to keep records, not tell us how to make loans."

"Does he do that? Tell you how to run your division?"

"No, of course not, but if he were president. You know better than I how important the loan division's role is to our success. Charlie's a strong loan man, and I want to keep the bank going in the same direction."

"You said Tony didn't understand loans. Do you understand deposits?"

"I spent a year in the training program, and much of that on the deposit side. I'm sure there are areas I'd have to brush up on, but in the main, I feel I could handle it. Loans are where the dollars are generated. The other divisions are, in a way, support functions of my division."

"Interesting observations, Ted. I appreciate you talking so frankly. Our talk has been very enlightening. I certainly agree good loans are important." George left Ted's office. He had much to ponder.

Chapter 23

A few minutes after George's visit, Ted left the bank and drove home. Entering the kitchen, he noted his mail laying on the counter, brought from the box by Mabel Harris, who he employed on a weekly basis to clean his home and iron his clothing. Thursday was her scheduled cleaning day, but she was available on the rare occasions he entertained guests. She was a conscientious worker, and he had retained her services for more than five years. He flipped on the light, selected a beer from the refrigerator, gathered up the loose mail and sat down at the table in the alcove. Thumbing through the letters he noticing a long, legal-sized envelope with embossed initials in the upper left-hand corner: *IICI, Honolulu, Hawaii*. His pulse quickened as he tore open the flap and removed a letter and two photostats stapled together. A circular logo in the upper left of the heavy bond stationery showed a drawing of Diamond Head and curved beach beneath. Adjacent was the bold blue lettering: "Inter-Island Construction, Inc." Beneath that, "Headquarters in Honolulu. Offices in Wailuku and Hilo."

> *Dear Mr. Jaffey,*
> *Enclosed are two documents bearing your signature. We request prompt payment of both so we may clear your account prior to end of our fiscal year. Your check in the amount of thirty-seven thousand dollars ($37,000.00) will be greatly appreciated.*
> *Sincerely,*
> *Douglas Young, President*

He reread the curt message in disbelief, then turned to the attached copies. His heart sank as he realized the pending difficulty he was in. First, he had failed to retrieve his original IOU for $12,000.00, and second, in his drunken state, he failed to note the two-year repayment clause in the marker for $25,000.00 was omitted. Both markers were demand notes. He threw the papers on the table in disgust, angry with Young for what he was attempting to perpetrate, angry with himself for being so easily duped. *Honorable man, my ass!* Ted thought angrily. *If he hadn't set me up and forced me to sign those markers...* He rose and began to pace, pausing occasionally to look out at a now-steady white curtain of snow enveloping the yard and shrubs. He tried to think clearly, but his mind continued to focus on the hate and contempt building against Young. *I just won't pay, it's that simple. These are gambling debts, not collectable in a court of law. Young can take his dirty little tricks and shove 'em!* Deep down, Ted knew that dismissal of the problem was not the simple solution he would like to pretend. He also knew he could be in a great deal of trouble if an answer could not be found, and quickly. That night he tossed and turned fitfully, mulling solution after solution. Toward morning he formulated a plan which, while risky, might solve his dilemma. He fell asleep, the seeds to his freedom more clearly planted in his mind. It was a gamble with some tough odds, but if successful, the rewards would be worth the risk and more.

Ted knocked at Flynn's office door and entered. "Working up the final figures on the Reardon Housing Project for loan committee," Flynn said.

"This Reardon deal won't set back your and Gina's vacation plan to Hawaii, will it?"

"No, I've got it covered. Let's go, I think the committees waiting for us."

Later, the loan meeting over, George and Charlie entered Charlie's office. "I wanted to ask if you have a prime candidate for your replacement."

Charlie sat down and looked across at George. "Who would be

your choice?"

"Now, old friend, don't answer my question with a question," George said, smiling.

Charles returned George's smile, then answered, "It's an interesting dilemma we find ourselves in. Three, maybe four candidates, each with strengths both business and personal. The three would be Ed, Ted, and Flynn. I'm not including Tony because he says he not interested. He insists he enjoys what he's doing and I see no reason to saddle him with a job that may make him ineffective."

"So, of the three which one do you favor?"

"Ed Gilbert's position gives him a broad understanding of the bank. Jaffey is a strong loan man and has a good perspective of the bank's direction. Flynn certainly is a possibility, especially if the major stockholder and chairman felt that strongly enough about his son-in-law. I could live with Flynn as the first choice." Charlie laughed. "Now, the ball is back in your court."

"I've tried to separate my personal involvement with Flynn from the real needs of the bank. After all, its success affects my family's future and me substantially. In my visit with Flynn, he, too, is a strong advocate of a continued aggressive loan policy but expressed concerns about Ted. His analysis may be colored since Ted is his boss, but he pointed out concerns I and others have expressed."

"Such as?"

"Lack of managerial skills when it comes to subordinates, a driving need to be separated, apart, superior to them. I've noticed at times his failure to consider the needs and role of the other divisions. If he holds himself and his department in such high esteem now, God knows how he'd act as president. I think we could lose some fine employees and managers with him in the driver's seat. You know how strongly I feel about family and a team concept."

"Ted has been very loyal to me, and to the loan policies we've established." Charlie's voice had an edge of defensiveness. "I would still come down on Ted's side."

"Let's keep our discussions open for a while longer, we still have time to decide," George said.

"I've got an appointment across town, I'll walk with you to your car." Ed rose and moved toward the door. In the elevator, and as they entered the second floor hallway, Charlie was sharing his recommendation of Flynn as the bank's representative to an upcoming loan conference in San Francisco. George had agreed. As they passed Ted Jaffey's darkened office, Charlie said, "Good, then we agree on Flynn."

Inside his office Ted stood, hand still resting on the wall near the light switch he had used moments before. It was obvious to Ted the two had been talking about their selection for President; the Chairman would naturally agree with the selection of his son-in-law. Ted realized he must hurry to set his plan of the night before in action.

Chapter 24

At home, Ted placed Young's letter and copies of the IOUs in his wall safe tucked behind the bookshelves in his den, then made a long-distance call to Young. "I received your letter and the enclosures. Needless to say, I'm not happy with what you're trying to do."

"I'm sorry, Mister Jaffey, I don't understand?"

Ted controlled his temper. "Our agreement was to tear up the first marker, replace it with the one for twenty-five thousand dollars and allow me two years to repay."

"You're a banker, Mister Jaffey. Surely you wouldn't allow someone to borrow money without interest."

"For two weeks! It's bad enough you think you can charge that for two years!"

"Please, Mister Jaffey, as the old American proverb states, 'Buyer beware.' If you don't take time to read what you sign, it may lead to unpleasant circumstances."

There was a brief silence until Ted finally said, "What if I refuse to pay? After all, gambling debts are not—"

"Mister Jaffey!" Young's voice cut in, cold and sharp. "The documents would be very embarrassing to you in your position at the Freeland Bank, and I know of other ways to convince you, much more painful ways, if you insist."

Ted wondered for a fleeting moment how Young knew where he worked, then remembered he had talked openly with Barnes and Hartley at their first meeting in the casino lounge. "That sounds like a threat."

"It is, Mister Jaffey, believe me, it is." Young's tone was confident. "Now that that matter is resolved, when may I expect your check?"

"What would you say if I told you I had a plan to make you even more money, and help me, too?"

Young paused a short moment before answering. "I'm listening."

"I don't want to discuss it on the phone. When are you going to be stateside again?" Ted asked.

"I have business in Seattle on Friday."

"Good, I'll meet you there." They agreed on a time and place.

"I'll listen to your plan. If I like it, I'll consider adjusting our business arrangement. Good-bye, Mister Jaffey."

Shortly after eight o'clock the following Friday, Ted Jaffey knocked at the door of room 1430 in the beautiful and ornate landmark Olympic Hotel. Young answered the door. He seemed smaller than Ted remembered, perhaps it was the silk dressing gown Young was wearing.

"I'm just finishing dinner," Young said, touching the corners of his mouth with a napkin. "Please sit down."

Ted took a seat on a contour chair. On either wall a door led to a bedroom. *Why a two-bedroom suite?* Ted wondered. His question was quickly answered when the large, bulky figure of Bill Hartley entered and sat down.

"You mentioned you have a plan, Mister Jaffey?" Young's tone was one of cool detachment.

"As a gambler you may enjoy the game I'm about to propose."

"I don't play games, Mister Jaffey. Everything I do, I do for good, sound business reasons."

"If that's true, why did you hoodwink me into that card game? I'm a small fish in a very small pond."

"You are one of many 'fish' that my friends Hartley and Barnes have caught while 'trolling.' I have learned that controlling a large number of small fish is easier than one big fish. Small fish are more easily caught and sometimes used as bait for bigger fish. And if I tire of one," his eyes narrowed, a sinister smile momentarily played across his face, "I can rid myself of it quickly with little mess and little notice."

Ted's stomach churned; he felt cold and frightened. Hartley stirred, cracked his knuckles loudly, and laughed softly. Ted was coming to full realization of his peril.

"But we digress. Please go on," Young said.

Ted considered fleeing the scene. He could sell his house, perhaps borrow the money, whatever it took to be free of the web in which he was ensnared. Still, if his plan could succeed.... He plunged ahead, briefly outlining the situation at Freeland Bank, his desire to become president, his need to remove Flynn Donovan as his rival.

Young listened quietly, occasionally sipping his drink. "So you want me to help you become President of the bank?"

"Yes."

"You mentioned I could make substantially more than the amount you owe me?"

"Donovan and his wife will be on vacation in Hawaii soon." Ted reached inside his pocket. "I have their basic itinerary, hotel, and so forth listed here." He passed the information to Young, who glanced at it briefly, then placed it on the table beside him. "If you or one of your people 'accidentally' met the Donovans, created a situation which would excite Donovan into getting himself and the bank involved in a major loan, my plan will work."

"I see two major flaws already, Mister Jaffey. One, your bank can't make direct loans to an Hawaiian company; and two, I'm not going to put my reputation on the line for you for a few quick dollars."

"I've thought of that. We can loan to a Washington-based company that in turn can use the funds elsewhere. If you don't wish to be involved, use a straw man, one of your staff as the promoter. Let me detail it more carefully. Say we use Byrum as the straw man. He establishes a front or dummy construction company in Washington. My homework shows you own substantial ground here in the Islands. You may eventually have to deed over a piece of ground to the straw man to satisfy the Title Company and the bank that he is the legal titled owner. Since he's your man, I presume you can protect yourself sufficiently. Bankers get very greedy. If a loan looks gold-plated, they sometimes don't take obvious precautions. If your straw man submits a strong financial statement, even though it's basically false, his credit will look good. The land is in his name, the development plans appear realistic, and the loan is approved. Look, strong financial statements and an appraisal of the completed project and the project carries itself, the loan is made. Surely, you know a 'friendly' appraiser?"

"You are to be commended, you investigate your 'clients' as carefully as I." Young smiled. "Now, the big money, where does it come from?"

"The bank makes Barnes the loan. He starts development to justify a couple legitimate draws to pay his subcontractors. About a month or so into the project, he mails three or four false purchase agreements to the bank, showing how eager people are to buy the completed lots. Barnes moves the project completion date up and hires more subs. Based on the sales contracts, the bank advances more money, as much as one hundred, one hundred fifty thousand dollars for construction, Barns doesn't pay the subs and disappears, leaving the subs and the bank holding the bag!"

"The subs are going to attach against the land and tie it up."

"Sure, they will, but that's what we want."

"Explain."

"Well, you clear a hundred grand or so. That should be more than enough to square me with you. The bank must either pay the subs to clear the liens and finish the project, or wait a year and a half more and go through a costly foreclosure. You are, of course, exposed to losing the land you 'sold' to Barnes. You may want to ride in on your white horse and bail out the bank or the subs at fifty cents on the dollar, complete the project and make an additional profit."

"What happens to the straw man?" Bill asked.

"Since he had nothing to start with, and he can't be found, the bank must be satisfied with what it can recoup from the project, or Mister Young's buy-out."

"You will be there to support the project when it's presented?"

"Let's say I won't stop it. I'll probably raise a mild objection so Flynn is collared with the loan. He is discredited, you have your money, I'm off your hook and a bank president besides."

Young shrugged. "It's a gamble, perhaps not a bad one; we just may have a deal. I'll review it and get back to you."

"You'll have to hurry. Flynn's vacation starts next week."

"I'll decide over the weekend and let you know," Young said.

Chapter 25

Flynn, Gina and Barnes met for lunch at the Royal Hawaiian Hotel. Barnes had manufactured a "chance" meeting with Flynn two days before on the beach, had outlined a project he had in mind and had mentioned he was looking for a bank to back him. Indicating he was headquartered in Seattle, he had hoped to obtain financing from a Washington bank. Flynn was immediately taken with the prospect of expanding the bank's investment horizons and, upon seeing the proposed site, was more convinced it was a worthwhile venture.

Anna and Steve had flown to Honolulu from Maui that morning so joined the threesome at the hotel. Barnes displayed some rough engineer drawings and an appraisal indicating the project worth two million dollars when completed, with an estimated marketing time of two years.

"I'm looking for a million, two hundred thousand for construction, does that seem feasible?"

"Based on what you've shown me, I'd be glad to recommend we support the loan. We'll have to have documentation, financial statements, et cetera, but we can discuss the details next week; for now I want to relax and enjoy our vacation." Upon his return to Aurora, Flynn brought glowing reports of Barnes' proposal and requested preliminary approval to issue a loan commitment.

Ed Gilbert indicated concern for committing such a large sum to an unknown contractor in an area far removed from their local region. Flynn countered that the Islands was a rapidly growing market and he had a verbal promise from a Honolulu title company to make periodic inspections for Freeland in return for the initial title order. In addition, because Barnes was to make an up-front loan fee deposit of fifteen thousand dollars, some of the money could be used to send a loan representative to visit the site, if needed. "Barnes tells me he has options on other properties. If we perform well on this loan, we'll have opportunities for additional business," Flynn added. "Give me the chance to present the full package before finally deciding; I'll have it ready in a few days." The loan committee agreed.

Ted was delighted; his plot to rid himself of his debt to Young and discredit Flynn was falling into place. Privately he indicated reservation with the project to Flynn, but maintained a moderate, uncommitted position at the loan committee meetings.

Young's telephone call to Jaffey a week following Flynn's presentation disrupted Ted's euphoric state. "I'm withdrawing my support—it's too risky and potentially too costly to me. Kill the deal."

Ted argued to no avail.

"If you stop and think, Mister Jaffey, you can still become a hero. By discrediting Flynn, your presidency still may be assured. As to the debt, that can be better resolved with you as president. I'm sure other opportunities will present themselves."

The implied further involvement did not escape Jaffey. "I'll have to expose Barnes and how he got the land. That puts you in the spotlight," Jaffey rallied, still hoping to change Young's decision.

"Go ahead. Even if the bank wanted to pursue Barnes, which I seriously doubt, he will not be found. As to the land, I protected myself by placing the title in escrow. My company was prepared to transfer property subject to full payment at closing. My company buys and sells property all the time; for Barnes' deal to have fallen apart is in the normal course of my business. Take care to kill this loan or your Board will know much more about your Las Vegas trip than you would wish. Do I make myself clear?"

More threats, Jaffey noted. Young's control of him was formidable.

The next morning Ted called an unscheduled loan meeting. All were in attendance, including Flynn and George.

"Gentlemen, let me get directly to the point of this meeting. The Hawaii project is dead. Flynn, in your initial talks with Barnes and based on his financial statement, how long did he say he owned the property?"

"Since 1952 or '53, I believe. I don't have the file with me."

"While you were in Honolulu did you review the title to be sure?"

"No, I presumed a preliminary title report will show he owns it. What's this all about?"

"There is no Barnes Construction Company filed in the State of Washington. There is no credit report information on his company or him here or in Hawaii. The title to the land is still vested with a major land holding company called 'Inter-Island Construction Incorporated' with clear title since 1946; the "appraiser" is not listed in the Honolulu phone book and the telephone number on his letterhead is an answering service. I'm told he hasn't used their services for over two years." He placed his notes in a folder and sat back.

"It would appear we were the target for a major swindle," Wesslin said. "How long did it take you to gather your facts, Ted?"

"A couple hours, a few phone calls."

"You could...no, should, have done all these things up front, Flynn," Wesslin said, an edge in his voice. "I went out on a limb by asking Northwest for a participation loan. I can't condone your unprofessional approach. We owe Ted our gratitude for saving us from, if not the actual swindle, at least the embarrassment for our management team and potential losses to our stockholders and Northwest Bank."

"I agree with Charlie. An explanation is in order. It appears your interest in this loan is tainted," Ted said.

"Tainted!" Flynn exploded, his Irish temper getting the better of him.

"Calm down, Flynn!" George's voice rose, anger displayed in his command. "Don't say something you'll later regret. Just shut your damn mouth. You and I will talk later."

"Yes, sir." Flynn sat back, his face red with humiliation.

Chapter 26

"Mister Young? Ted Jaffey. My plan worked splendidly; I don't think Donovan has a prayer. Even old man Stern is disenchanted with him. My chance for president has improved. Now, I assuming since I protected you on this Barnes deal you will forget the debt. I want my markers."

"Come Jaffey, don't be naive. If you want your markers, pay me off, it's that simple."

Ted thought quickly, then asked, "What if I could present you a plan to take over the bank by becoming its major stockholder, would that satisfy the debt?"

"Another plan, Mister Jaffey? You are resourceful if nothing else! Own a bank? Yes, I'd be interested, providing it was done with no legal repercussions against me."

"It's rather complicated; we'd need another meeting. When will you be in Seattle again?"

"I have no need to return to the Northwest, but I'd be glad to discuss your new idea with you here on the Islands. You may stay at my home a few days, relax, talk through your plan. Let me know of your decision." The line went dead.

Ted had no plan for a stock takeover; control of Freeland was too heavily vested in the Stern family, but he was tired of dealing with Young. A bolder plan must be put into motion.

Wesslin granted Ted's wish to take a vacation. After a quick call to Young, Ted drove to Seattle and purchased an airline ticket. His plane landed in Honolulu Saturday afternoon.

"Hi, Ted, over here!" Barnes spoke briefly to a woman who turned and left, then Barnes walked to Ted, hand outstretched. "Let's get your bags and get out of here."

They drove along the highway adjacent to the beach and resort hotels, then climbed the low hills east of Honolulu, eventually pulling into a long driveway leading to a handsome two-story house commanding a magnificent view of the city and harbor. Behind, Diamond Head towered above them.

"Ah, Mister Jaffey. Welcome to my home." Douglas Young said, greeting Ted just outside the front door. "Come in. I have a few friends here. Mister Barnes, of course, Mister Hartley, and my companion, Miss Lisa."

Lisa was more gorgeous than Ted remembered—black hair loose, hanging down her back, a royal blue two-piece bathing suit accentuating her long legs and narrow waist.

"Hello, Mista Jaffey." She smiled politely.

He looked for a sign of tenderness or affection, but detected none. Surely the note, that evening in his room, implied a mutual understanding.

"I read your note," he said to her.

"A nice touch, don't you think?" Young smiled. "My fish often find solace in them—something to pique their egos."

Ted understood more fully the lengths to which the four had gone in staging his entrapment.

"Question. Why didn't you wait and then repurchase the property as we discussed? I'm sure the bank would have considered a bail-out early on."

"I saw no reason to arouse suspicion with your bank. An offer from the previous owner to repurchase land he had just sold might lead to too much snooping. Your plan may have been revealed. Besides, I intend to do more business with your bank in the future. I'd even be prepared to give back your markers if I accept this new plan you mentioned on the telephone."

Ted frowned. "Still playing your little games, aren't you?"

Young smiled, then changed the subject. "You must be tired from your trip. Perhaps a shower and change of clothes would be welcome.

Mister Hartley, see Mister Jaffey to his room. We eat at six. Be casual; we don't dress for dinner. Afterward we'll talk, maybe watch some movies."

"Sounds fine to me," Ted answered, knowing any attempt to alter the present situation futile. A shower and a nap would help him relax. The thought Lisa might join him crossed his mind, but he realized that was wishful thinking; perhaps it could be arranged later.

The house was cool as compared to the heat of outdoors. The structure, built shortly after the war, featured teak and mahogany woods, tile and wood parquet floors, a generous use of windows, a red California tile roof. An open stairway led to a wide hallway extending the length of the second floor, allowing entrance to the bedrooms that overlooked the gardens and ocean view. The main floor contained a spacious living area with rich Oriental carpeting, a modern kitchen, a dining area, an office, a small theater and projection room, laundry and pantry facilities, and a three-car garage. Palm and eucalyptus trees plus undergrowth of native ferns, moss, and lichens surrounded the veranda. At the far end, near the edge of the steep slope, a sparkling swimming pool and waterfall provided an attractive center for entertainment and barbecuing.

Ted was led to a comfortable room with adjoining bath. Louvered wooden doors opened to a small, private balcony on which one could sunbathe, read, or enjoy the splendid view.

"Very nice."

"We like it."

"Do you all live here?"

"Most of the time. The boss's suite is at the far end of the hallway. Barnes's is next to him, then my room, and the two guest rooms."

"Lisa?"

Hartley laughed. "With the boss, of course."

"Of course," Ted said.

Ted unpacked, carefully hanging his lightweight slacks and shirts in the closet. Other than the heavier sport jacket he had worn on the airplane, he had brought his summer-weight pale blue blazer and one tie. He spread his toiletries on the marble counter top in the bath, noticing the shower was constructed of small individual tiles less than an inch square. Mr. Young lived first-class, Ted conceded. The last item Ted removed from his suitcase was a snub-nose .38 revolver purchased at a pawnshop on First Avenue in Seattle shortly before boarding the plane. Using tape from his first-aid kit, he secured the weapon to the underside of the nightstand. If they searched his room, it would not be readily found. He showered, then lay on the open bed, the shuttered balcony door partially open, the pungent odors of the tropics filtering into the room. Far away, Ted could hear the waves pounding on the shore. He fell asleep.

"Mista Jaffey," Lisa's said as her warm hand touched his shoulder. "Mista Jaffey, it's time to get up."

He opened his eyes. Her beautiful face was bent close to his, her black hair touching his arm. He awoke slowly, noticing someone had covered his naked body with the bed sheet. "Did you do this?" he asked, glancing down.

"Do what?"

"Cover me. You didn't like what you saw?" he teased, searching her face for a hint of shared desire.

"Yes. I liked very much...but...Mista Young would not be happy if I—"

"If you what?" He reached for her, forcing her down on the bed beside him. She did not resist nor did she encourage him; her wide-set eyes merely stared back passively. "You must get tired of sleeping with a skinny old man."

"I came to tell you dinner is ready, that is all," Lisa said coolly. "Please, you will come now?"

"Sure. Sure. Tell them I'll be along shortly. Now get out of here, so I can get dressed." *Bitch,* Ted said to himself.

Chapter 27

After a relaxing dinner, they moved to the terrace to watch the last rays of the sun disappear as darkness descended quickly. Small oil-soaked torches were lighted and placed in stands around the perimeter of the patio and near the pool, the shadows dancing against the water and dense, forested background.

Ted sipped his wine and turned to Young. "Something you said earlier interests me."

"What is that, Mister Jaffey?"

"You indicated you would be doing more business with our bank. How?"

"Borrowings. Small loans, nothing elaborate."

"That's ridiculous, I'd never loan you any money!"

"Let me explain, please. Remember I told you about my school of small fish?"

"Yes."

"My school consists of several bankers, such as yourself, scattered here and there, mostly on the West Coast. They, too, found a gambling debt or personal loan too large to repay—or perhaps the love of a woman, drugs, whatever his source of indiscretion. But you, Mister Jaffey, are more enterprising than the others. You had a plan that would reward us both handsomely and retire your debt. You are to be congratulated on your ingenuity; unfortunately it didn't succeed."

"Perhaps, but this little fish may still get away."

"Yes? That is yet to be determined. My system is very simple and basically foolproof. My fish make small, unsecured loans—a simple demand note for five to ten thousand dollars—to imaginary, and as it turns out, disreputable clients. The bank writes off the loan against bad debts and I am the recipient of the funds. We aren't gluttons. We rotate the assignments. Only a few of my banker friends work for me at any one time, but it does produce a nice tax-free income each year. Young smiled. "Enough about business. Do you like movies, Mister Jaffey? I have some film I'm sure will interest you. Good shows are so hard to come by on the Islands. Mister Barnes has prepared the projection room. Bring your drinks if you wish."

Ted felt Lisa beside him, her body pressed against him softly. "You may sit with me if you wish," she whispered, holding him back for a moment as the others went inside.

"With them in the room? I'm not crazy. If they though we were getting out of line, Hartley could crush me like a grape."

"It will be dark, no one need know but you and me. Then later, when the old man is asleep...." Her hand squeezed his, then she moved ahead to join the others.

The theater was small, with a dozen comfortable chairs. "This is one of my favorite rooms," Young said. "At night, if I can't sleep, I come here and watch a movie. I made it soundproof so as not to disturb the others."

The lights dimmed to total darkness. Before the bright shaft of light exploded against the screen, Ted felt Lisa slide onto the chair beside him, her hand seeking his leg.

"You'll enjoy this as much as I do," she whispered.

Ted watched with fascination as the camera panned across a hotel room, then focused on the naked body of a young woman. Long, supple legs, small waist, long black hair—it was Lisa. She turned to the camera, the subdued light making exciting peaks and valleys across her soft skin. She smiled and moved to the bed. The camera moved with her to the bed, revealing the naked body of a man.

"Jesus!" Ted yelled. "That's me!"

Ted realized Hartley had sat down behind him. Lisa now lay back against the chair arm, leaning away from him. On the screen, Lisa was making love to the near inert body, her fingers and mouth managing to achieve an erection of Ted's member. She rolled on him, then rolled him on top of her legs thrown apart and around him, their bodies moving up and down in rhythm. The camera came closer, showing her head thrown back, her tongue caressing her lips, a look of excitement on her face, then pleasure. Even in his horror and anger he could see he contributed little or nothing to the performance. On screen, he rolled off her as the camera focused on her, kissing his face and chest. She moved from camera range as another form came into focus—a young boy of twelve or thirteen.

"My God!" Ted hissed. The boy appeared to perform a sexual act with Ted, the camera concentrating on the boy's head going up and down, Ted's body rolling slightly, moving in cooperation. Then the boy left, as the camera panned from Ted's now limp member to his torso and sleeping face, then fade out.

"So, Mister Jaffey, it would seem our business relationship is not so easily ended after all?" Young's voice was a grating sound that Ted was fast coming to hate. His mouth was dry, his heart pounding like an African drum.

"You dirty bastard," Ted yelled.

Hartley's fist slammed onto the back of Ted's skull, rendering him nearly unconscious. His body limp, he fell forward onto the carpet with a heavy thud.

"Enough, Mister Hartley," Young said calmly. "Get our guest to his room. And Mister Jaffey, after you leave here, please don't think of doing something foolish like going to the police. It is surprising who and what money can buy."

Half-walking, half-dragged, Ted staggered up the stairs to his room with the help of Hartley and Barnes. They threw him on the bed, his head still ringing from Hartley's sledgehammer blow.

"As the boss said, be a good boy. I'll be outside to be sure you stay that way. By the way, it's almost thirty feet to the patio. Don't be a fool. We lost one who tried," Hartley said.

Hartley went out, and Ted heard the key turn in his door. From down the hallway, "Good night, Teddy," a seductive voice came from the hall. It was Lisa. "I told you it was great!" He could hear her laughing all the way to Young's room.

Chapter 28

He lay on the bed, drifting in and out of consciousness. Later, as his head cleared, the pain in his neck and shoulders eased. Crossing to the door, he turned the knob—still locked. He listened, ear pressed against the door. He detected the slow, labored breathing of Hartley.

He risked turning on a small night light in the bathroom. Between the reflected glow from the light and the moon, he gained his bearings. Carefully, he opened the closet and dresser drawers. His room had been searched—nothing obvious: a telltale corner of his boxer shorts bent under, the clothing slightly twisted on their hangers. Fortunately the revolver was still under the bedside table. He removed it carefully, the ripping away of the tape sounding loud and clear in Ted's ears. Carefully he opened the chamber, noting the five bullets were still in place.

He had to get away, and surprise was his best ally. If he could render Hartley unconscious without alerting the others...but how? A shot would wake the entire household. Again he visited the bathroom. Using his pocketknife, he cut a wash cloth into strips. From his shirt collars he extracted four stays and taped them at even distance around the barrel, the ends sticking out past the opening. Being vigilant not to obstruct the aperture, he wrapped the strips of wash cloth around the stays and barrel, securing each layer with tape until he had approximately three-quarters of an inch of soft insulation. To what extent his makeshift silencer would work he did not know, but if it diminished the discharge noise to any degree, it would serve his immediate purpose.

He took two deep breaths and walked to the door. "Hartley!" he called out in a stage whisper. "I need a doctor, I'm bleeding from my ears. I can't see! Help me!"

"Shit!"

Ted hurried back to his bed and lay down as he heard the key turn and the door open. Lying on his stomach, revolver tucked under him, he watched through half-closed eyes as Hartley lumbered toward him. That he had been asleep was evident in his walk.

"Turn on the light, I can't see!" Ted said in a low voice.

The overhead light filled the room with brightness; Hartley momentarily blinded.

Quickly Ted rolled to his side and pointed the gun at Hartley's stomach.

"What the...!"

"Now don't say a word. Just stay quiet while I get out of here. Open your mouth, and you're a dead man." Ted kept the gun trained on Hartley as he put the last of his clothing into his suitcases and snapped them shut.

"Car keys?"

"Young's room."

"Bullshit, you must have some. Empty out your pockets!"

"Now don't get excited. You might hurt someone with that peashooter."

"Just give me the damn keys and stop stalling."

"Sure, here!" Hartley threw them hard and sprang after them, taking Ted off guard for a moment. Hartley was two steps away when Ted pulled the trigger. The bullet struck the on-rushing giant in the center of his chest, blood spurting, then spreading across the flowers on his shirt. Hartley's momentum carried him past Ted, and he landed heavily on the floor and lay still. The gunshot had been muffled substantially.

Ted listened intently but heard nothing from down the hall. Retrieving the keys and replacing the spent bullet in the empty chamber, he started for the stairs, then realized that his freedom would not come by fleeing Young's home. As long as the film and negatives existed, he would always be under his control. He knew what he must do. Quietly, he moved across the downstairs and out to the large Lincoln Continental parked in the garage, opened the trunk and placed his bags inside, closing the lid silently. Finding the telephone box, he cut the wires with his knife.

Back inside, he moved stealthily upstairs. In his room, Hartley remained prone on the floor, no sign of life. He crept past Barnes's room and pushed open the door to Young's suite. The dim light showed him asleep on one bed, while on the other, naked and nearly uncovered, Lisa lay curled in deep sleep.

Ted tiptoed to Young's bedside. Placing the revolver inches from Young's temple, he whispered, "Wake up, you sonnavabitch."

Startled, Young opened his eyes. "Mister Jaffey? What time is it?"

"Later than you think, old man. Get up."

"All right. I don't know what you intend to do, but it won't work. Hartley and Barnes will take care of you, gun or no gun."

"Hartley already tried, and failed."

Young's eyes flew open, then quickly returned to normal.

"Now call Barnes in here. Try anything, and you get it first."

Lisa was awake now, listening, starting to piece together what was happening.

"Lisa, go tell Barnes I want to see him," Young said.

"No, you call him in here. Nobody leaves this room."

"Mister Barnes! Come here, please!" Young called out.

A sleepy Barnes entered, barefoot, his bathrobe half tied, squinting against the light Ted had turned on.

"We have company. Mister Jaffey is, at the moment, holding all the cards."

"Hartley will hear us. He'll take care of you, smart guy," Barnes said, sizing up the situation.

"Mister Jaffey tells me Mister Hartley is dead."

Ted motioned with the revolver. "I know how to use this and I will. Now, you three, up, and down the stairs."

They filed out, Young in a silk bathrobe, Barnes in his terry cloth, Lisa in a thin, short nightgown she'd had laying at the foot of her bed. At the bottom of the stairs Young stopped.

"The theater. Go in and turn on the lights and make yourselves comfortable," Ted directed.

"You want the film and your markers? No problem. Mister Barnes, get them for me, please."

"Sit down," Ted snarled.

"He's going to kill us!" Lisa said. "Teddy, not me! We can go away, I be good for you, you will like me!" She slipped out of her gown and started toward him.

His eyes momentarily on her, Ted nearly missed Barnes's quick sprint toward him. Ted dodged sideways, his athletic skills coming to his rescue. He shot Barnes behind the left ear, knocking him into a nearby chair.

"Now, you two! Back down to the far end of the room! And drag your friend with you."

"Please don't shoot us. I don't want to die, please! I'll do anything, anything!" Lisa whined.

"You make it sound tempting, but no thanks. I'm tired of your prick-teasing games." His next slug found Lisa's left breast. The hole created the momentary illusion of her having double nipples, then her life began draining away, dark and red over her torso.

What made Ted turn at that moment, he would never know—perhaps a draft on his back, a sudden glance from Young. He whirled as Hartley staggered toward him, arms outstretched like a drunken monster, his entire shirt and front soaked with blood, half-choking sounds issuing from his gaping mouth. Ted fired. The bullet hit Hartley between the eyes, making a clean, neat hole in the tanned flesh. Hartley's body jerked backward from the impact, hit the steps of the sunken floor, and rolled one, two, three times before coming to rest on his back, staring up through sightless eyes.

Young was cowering in the corner, speechless. "A quick death is too good for you!" Ted yelled. He walked slowly forward, a mask of pure hate across his face. Taking careful aim, he spent his last shells on each of Young's kneecaps, bringing him helpless and screaming in pain to a fetal position. Ted ran from the room. With all the strength he could muster, he shoved a large mahogany chest across the door, blocking any attempt to exit.

On the veranda, Ted lit several torches; then, starting in the upstairs bedroom area, he made his way room to room, then down the stairs and through the main floor, igniting drapes and shutters as he went. Retreating to the garage, he started the Lincoln and roared down the driveway. In the rear view mirror, he saw the house erupt into a roaring inferno as the stained woods and painted surfaces caught and spread—the tile roof acting as a lid to contain the fire inside. A few blocks away, he pulled the car to the curb and waited as several fire engines roared by, sirens wailing. The entire horizon glowed with the intensity of the now engulfed structure. He drove toward the outskirts of town and pulled the Lincoln into the parking lot of a small building with a faded FOR SALE OR LEASE sign tacked on the front door.

Carefully, he wiped the steering wheel, door handles, dashboard, and trunk free of fingerprints. It was nearly five a.m., and early morning traffic was starting to move along the main streets. Luggage in hand, he walked to a nearby motel, hailed a cab, and asked for the airport.

He had dropped the gun in a storm sewer drain several blocks from the house. He moved to the ticket counter of Northwest Orient and stood patiently in line. Later, as the plane circled after takeoff, he looked toward Diamond Head, seeing a grey wisp of smoke rising from a blackened area on the side of the low hills.

Aloha, Mr. Young, he said to himself. A feeling of accomplishment lifted his spirits. He felt not a moment's remorse.

Chapter 29

Flynn's attitude and personality showed marked changes following the Barnes land development scandal. While the bank suffered little harm to its reputation and no monetary loss, the community reacted negatively to the leaked suggestions of Flynn's apparent indiscretion. Despite the philanthropic and community involvement of the Stern family, some found comfort that a leading citizen's son-in-law may have been tempted into a white-collar crime. The efforts to squelch the rumors, including an editorial lashing of the rumormongers in the Aurora Advocate, had small impact on its readers. He became withdrawn, his relationship with bank employees and family subdued, often verging on being sullen and curt. Gina was not able to comfort him, to share with him as in the past. Their marital relationship was strained and distant.

He had been deeply hurt by Ted Jaffey's insinuation that his support of the project may have been tainted, suggesting a kickback. Even his father-in-law seemed less supportive and avoided the open, frank relationship he had savored. Jaffey continued to make Flynn's life a living hell. The continued innuendoes regarding his lack of prudent underwriting, his repeated assignments to menial tasks more representative of a beginning clerk's duties, were a difficult adjustment. The rumor persisted among the employees that Flynn would have benefitted financially from the project.

Flynn sat on the edge of the bed leaning forward, his head in his hands. "Maybe I should quit. This nonsense of my receiving money under the table hurts most of all."

"It will blow over," Gina said. "You know people suspect the worst sometimes."

"Ted's been my biggest detractor. I wouldn't be surprised if he wasn't the author of the ugly rumors."

"Look, you need to get away. I was going to Seattle for a couple days with Janet and Babs. Let me cancel and you and I go instead."

"No. You go. It will give me a chance to think things out." He slumped down, tears welling in his eyes. "You'd be better off if I wasn't even around."

"Don't say that! What would we do without you?" She stroked his back and rubbed his shoulders. "You'll see, things will get better. By the way, I told Margaret she could stay overnight at Joyce's Friday—slumber party with some of the gang."

Friday evening Flynn returned to a dark house. The afternoon mail lay on the entrance table with a note from Margaret reminding him of her slumber party. He discovered a letter and some clippings from Anna. He scanned them quickly. Among the items mentioned was a forthcoming sailing trip to the South Seas in connection with a film on which she and Steve were working. The location would make it difficult for anyone to contact them, but mail would be forwarded from time to time. Flynn read the P.S. clippings with mounting interest.

"Enclosed clippings are from last week's Honolulu Herald. Is this the Mr. Barnes we had lunch with? I saw Barnes with Mr. Jaffey at the airport a day or two before the fire. (See clippings) They seemed in a hurry, and my old legs couldn't catch up to say hello. Write soon."

Barnes and Jaffey together! The impact of this information stunned Flynn. He sat down in the living room, anxious to read the news clippings:

FIRE ENGULFS LUXURY HOME

Firemen fought an early morning blaze that totally destroyed the luxurious home of wealthy landowner and developer, Douglas Young. The cause of the fire is under investigation. It is reported four bodies were found in the home, charred beyond recognition. The coroner's office is investigating for any clues that may have contributed to the victims' deaths other than the fire. Dental impressions and fingerprints will be examined by the local police with the aid of the FBI Crime Lab in Washington, D.C.

Fire officials are baffled as to what caused the fire, but unconfirmed reports suspect arson may be involved. Young was the president and founder of the Inter Island Construction, Incorporated (IICI).

IICI, Flynn remembered, was the owner of the property to be purchased by Barnes! Anna saw Jaffey and Barnes together. He quickly read the second article.

ARSON CONFIRMED—BODIES IDENTIFIED

Honolulu Fire Department officials today confirmed the cause of last Saturday's early morning fire which destroyed the half-million-dollar mansion of wealthy owner/developer, Douglas Young, to be man-caused. Battalion Chief Bobbie Keaau was quoted as saying, "We located several spots of origin; there is no doubt arson is involved." He would not comment further. Efforts by the police and FBI criminal labs have tentatively identified the dead as:

Young, the owner; William Hartley; Byrum Barnes; and Lisa Chung Yamato, all of this Island.

Inside Sources indicate both Barnes and Hartley have minor criminal records. Public records listed the Young house as Miss Yamato's home address. A possible link to the killer or killers' identification is Mr. Young's Lincoln Continental, discovered yesterday afternoon abandoned several miles from the fire. Police will not reveal what clues they have obtained from searching the vehicle. The investigation as to who started the fire and how and why the foursome came to die is the subject of intensive investigation, although reliable sources inside the Police Department indicate that at least three of the four occupants had been shot. Funeral and burial arrangements will be announced later. Young may have family in Australia, but so far this is unconfirmed. Barnes and Hartley reportedly have families in Texas. Miss Yamato's hometown is unknown.

Flynn had most of the pieces to a puzzle and was attempting to fit them together. He did not understand how Jaffey and the people in Hawaii came to meet. What he did realize was Jaffey's probable involvement in the scheme from its inception. Impulsively he shoved the letter and clippings into his overcoat pocket and bolted into the garage, almost forgetting to press the automatic door opener in his haste to get to Jaffey's house. He pulled into Jaffey's driveway in the gathering darkness of the late December evening. Ted, wearing a long-sleeved shirt and Levis, answered his knock on the door.

"Flynn, what brings you out on a late Friday evening?"

"These," Flynn said, his wrath almost beyond control, as he thrust the letter and clippings into Ted's startled face.

"What the hell are these?" Ted drew back as Flynn pushed his way past him into the living room.

"Read the letter and damn clippings." Flynn's anger mounted as his reasoning powers surrendering to his high mounting fury. Ted glanced at the clippings; his face turned ashen for a moment, then he was in control. "What do these have to do with me?"

"Everything—it's right there in the clipping! You were in on the Barnes deal from the beginning. You probably burned the house down! You probably killed the people, Barnes and...and the rest!"

"You're nuts! A fire happens three thousand miles away, and you blame me? You have flipped your top, Flynn. I have a mind to call the police and have you thrown out."

"The police? Go ahead, and call them—or should I? You'll have a hell of a time explaining this away."

"Hold up a minute. You're the one who met with Barnes. You're the one who fucked up the project, not me!"

Flynn could not believe Ted's attitude, his apparent ability to avoid the simple truth. Then he realized he had not told Ted the keystone to his knowledge. "You were seen with Barnes in Hawaii—a day or so before the fire. You going to deny that, too?"

"You're full of it, Flynn."

"Gina's aunt saw you in the airport. It's right there in her letter."

Ted blanched as he read the incriminating postscript. "Who else knows about this?"

"So you did do it! You're as much as admitting it! Tomorrow everyone will know; Wesslin, my father-in-law, the police, the whole town." Flynn shook his head in disgust. "God, Ted, I knew you were a no good bastard. But killing? Arson?"

"I asked who else knows about these?" Ted rattled the letter and clippings at Flynn.

"For the moment just us." Too late Flynn realized his foolishness; in his haste and anger to confront Jaffey, he had failed to call George or the police. Ted moved so quickly that Flynn had no time to react. His heavy overcoat added to his inability to counteract Ted's attack. Grabbing Flynn's neck in the crook of his right arm, Ted squeezed down hard, shutting off Flynn's air almost instantly. Flynn struggled vainly, but the lack of oxygen prevailed, and he slumped to the floor unconscious. Ted continued to apply pressure with his chokehold until Flynn's body became limp, his breathing apparently stopped. Ted hastily checked for a pulse, finding it shallow and slow. Donning his heavy parka, warm gloves, and snow boots, Ted stepped out into the cold, dark night. Quickly he lifted Flynn onto his shoulders and deposited the still limp body in the passenger seat of Flynn's sedan, then drove away. Ted quickly settled on a plan to rid himself of Flynn's body. He would make it appear Flynn had committed suicide. Ted knew Gina was away and Shawn and Michael not yet home for the Christmas vacation. That left Margaret; if necessary, he would have to deal with her, too.

Ted stopped two doors from Flynn's house. The two-story colonial was dark; apparently no one was home. Quickly, Ted open the automatic door, drove the car into the garage, and ran the door down again. He moved Flynn to an upright position behind the wheel. By the dome light, Ted examined Flynn's throat for possible bruises or marks and saw none. Flynn's heavy muffler had apparently cushioned the chokehold. Silently, Ted entered the house, turning on a small lamp in the entrance hall. He noticed Margaret's note to her father and knew he would be safe. In the pantry area he found the vacuum hose and from the laundry basket retrieved several soiled towels.

Returning to the garage, he packed the towels along the underside of the garage door, then carefully folded a towel against the door leading to the house. Flynn was still unconscious as Ted forced one end of the vacuum hose over the car's exhaust pipe and pushed the other end through a rear window, rolling the glass tight to clamp the hose between window and frame. Reaching inside, he started the car. The odor and fumes filled the car and garage quickly. Making sure the car windows were tightly shut, he stepped into the house and closed the door very slowly, allowing the towel to fall against the door. He retraced his steps inside the house, making certain nothing appeared disturbed. His last act was to turn off the hall lamp as he slipped quickly outside and to the sidewalk. The faint idling noise of Flynn's car in the garage concerned Ted, but he presumed few people would be out on such a cold night. Pulling the hood of the parka over his head, he strolled off into the night, a slight spring to his step. *I must take more walks,* he thought. *The fresh air is invigorating.*

Back in his garage, Flynn slumped forward then fell to one side.

Chapter 30

At George's request, Charlie had gone to the Homeplace Saturday morning for a hot roll, a cup of coffee, and "a chat," as George had put it.

The two men moved to the warmth of the living room, enjoying a third cup of coffee. Sitting by the fireplace, they watched the flames lick and encircle the aged pine logs, listened to the occasional snap and pop as heat burst a small pitch pocket, sparks jumping, as the logs glowed brighter for an instant.

"Charlie, we haven't decided on your replacement, and I know you want to announce your retirement effective year's end. I'd hoped you might wait a little longer, but you tell me that's not in the cards."

"I'm ready to back Gilbert."

"Good! We both agreed on Ed as your replacement, so that's no longer a problem."

They sat in silence a few minutes.

"This situation with Flynn bothers me. His attitude and lackluster approach to the job," George sighed.

"I've noticed. Part of dropping my support for Jaffey is the way he is making Flynn's life miserable. He won't let up on the Hawaiian fiasco. Frankly, I hope Ed asks for Ted's resignation."

"You've certainly changed your tune since last spring." George smiled.

"I have, and I'll be the first to admit it. I've been watching Ted more carefully, listening to what he says, observing him. You're right. He's a damn yes-man and a poor manager. I plan on making the formal announcement of Ed Gilbert appointment on Monday and a prepared release for the media. Maybe Ted will leave on his own.

Let's hope so."

At that moment the ringing of the telephone interrupted the conversation. George strolled to the telephone and answered. At first, he believe the caller to be a prankster, speaking gibberish—but a hint of recognition in the voice, the tone, made him pause and not hang up.

"Margaret? Is that you, dear? Stop crying. Tell me what's wrong."

"Gram...Grampa...and I opened...and...and...the car...it's Daddy!" She broke down again, wailing into the mouthpiece.

"Please, dear, get hold of yourself." George hoped his voice did not reveal his anxiety. He placed his hand over the mouthpiece, "My granddaughter—she's hysterical. I can't...Yes, Margaret, I'm right here, dear."

"Come quick. Daddy's—Daddy's dead!"

"My God, child! What are you saying?"

"Please, just come!"

"You at home?"

"Yes."

"I'll be right over. Hang on!"

"George, you're white as a sheet." Charlie rushed to his friend's side. "What's happened?"

"I don't know exactly. Margaret said her daddy is dead!"

"Flynn?"

"Yes. I must go to her." He hurried to the closet for his coat. "Do me a favor, Charlie?"

"Anything."

"Call the police and tell them to meet me at Flynn's house. Then call the Ben Franklin in Seattle—Gina is staying there. Tell her to come as quickly as possible. If not there, leave a message to call here, not home. Understand?"

"Will do."

"One more thing. Please stay here until I call you. You can tell me about Gina, and I may have you make some other calls."

Following the call to the police department, Charles contacted the hotel in Seattle and was told Gina and party had checked out shortly after nine o'clock. The clerk indicated she had left to avoid a predicted snowstorm in the mountain passes.

Charles had no more than hung up when another call rang through.

"Stern residence."

"Charlie, did you get in touch with Gina?"

"She's apparently on her way. What's happening there?"

"I can't talk long, the police are here and Margaret's still in shock. I called Doc Lehrman to come by. It looks like suicide."

"My God, how?"

"Carbon monoxide. He ran a hose into his car. Towels stuffed under the garage doors. It's awful. The coroner just walked in, I'll have to go. Would you do a couple more favors? I hate to ask, but I must stay here."

"Sure."

"Call Mike and Shawn at school. Tell them to come home. The phone numbers are in my telephone directory in the den. Also, call Steve and Anna Northshield on Maui. Their numbers are in my directory, too. Tell Steve and Anna it isn't necessary they come at once—they are to wait for my call."

"I'll get right on it."

"Thanks, Charlie."

Charles relayed the sad news to Shawn and Mike, indicated their father was dead, not detailing the circumstances. His last call was to Anna. "Hello, Missus Northshield? This is Charles Wesslin in Aurora. Do you remember me?"

"Yes, of course I remember you." She paused, a catch in her voice. "Is my brother all right?"

"Oh, yes, George is fine, but I do have some distressing news, I'm afraid. Your nephew, Flynn, was found dead this morning, an apparent suicide."

"Suicide! I can't believe it! The rest of the family, how are they holding up?"

Charles explained the circumstances of the last hour. "By the way, George asked you not to make plans to come here until you've talked with each other."

"This is awful. Hang on a minute, please. I need to discuss something with my husband."

Several minutes passed before Anna came back on the line. "I hate to say this, but it would be very difficult to come even if George asked me to. I will if he insists, of course, but we have equipment, a ship, staff—a tight, tight schedule to meet. It's a film project that's taken us nearly a year to put together. Oh, God, this is so upsetting!"

"Perhaps you could catch up to your ship later," Charlie suggested.

"No—that's the terrible part. We'll be in open seas the better part of a month, and then we're stopping at ports of call that can't accommodate commercial airlines."

"Shall I tell George you're not coming and explain, or...how do you want to handle it?" Charles asked.

"I'd never forgive myself if I don't talk to him. Tell him to call, keep calling until he gets us, no matter how late."

Chapter 31

The suicide of Flynn Donovan created mixed reactions. For his family and closest friends, shock and disbelief. Others, fed by the ugly rumors of possible scandal associated with the land swindle, nodded wisely. Whispers of "I could've told you so," and, "This just proves what I suspected all along," were bantered about. The police and coroner's investigation listed the death as suicide. Only the cryptic notation, "No suicide note found" under 'Remarks' on the detective's report would suggest the death anything other than routine.

Gina agonized over Flynn's death. Following the initial shock and numbness and the morbid pageantry of the funeral, her anger and frustration turned against Ted Jaffey.

"I'm surprised Ted didn't offer to shovel the dirt into the grave, that bastard!" Gina fumed.

"A vendetta isn't going to help. Don't let this bitterness control you. It won't bring Flynn back," George said, concerned about his daughter's growing obsession.

"Dad, you really don't know the hurt and cruelty he brought to Flynn's life. Just days before he died, Flynn cried in my arms, telling me how Jaffey was belittling him, putting him down, making his job a living hell. He thought Jaffey had started the rumor about the under-the-table money."

"I've heard the same rumors, but it's speculation. You have no proof."

"You're right, but you certainly know Ted was jealous of Flynn. The way the staff went to him with their troubles, the respect he had inside and outside the office, those types of things. Maybe I should confront Jaffey and find out for myself."

"I wouldn't recommend that, but if you do, be careful. He can charm the birds out of the trees when he wants to. Eventually, most people see through him."

"Apparently not everyone, he's still a division manager. Call it woman's intuition or whatever you may choose, but no one will ever convince me Ted didn't push Flynn over the edge. But there is some payback. Wesslin's announcement that Ed Gilbert was appointed president must have made Jaffey a very angry and unhappy individual." A look of contempt crossed her face. "It couldn't happen to a nicer guy." Gina's jaw set in a firm line; her eyes fired with the growing desire for revenge. "I'm still going to see he gets his!"

It was shortly after the Christmas holidays. Ted was in his office when he heard voices from the outer office, one raised in anger, the other—Frances, his secretary—speaking in calmer but pleading tones.

"What's going on out here?" he asked, throwing open the door.

"I'm sorry, Mister Jaffey. Missus Donovan insisted on seeing you, and I ..."

"I want to talk to you and no little piece of fluff is going to stop me!" Gina said.

"Calm down, Gina. If you must, come in."

As she entered, Ted closed the door and sat down, placed his fingertips together, eyes narrowed, and waited.

"I want you to know just what I think of you. I want to look my husband's killer straight in the eye and tell him what a sonnavabitch I think he is!"

Ted remained outwardly calm. *Surely she couldn't know anything!* He waited, gathering his thoughts.

"You couldn't let up, could you? You hounded him, belittled him, cut him down until he couldn't stand it anymore. You killed Flynn just as much as if you had put the hose in the car yourself!"

Ted tensed; she was speaking the truth but did not know it. He had weighed the danger Anna Northshield presented him and had considered killing her, but for him to disappear at the same time of

Flynn's suicide might have drawn undue attention. Then he'd heard Anna was not coming to the funeral and, in fact, was off on an extended project at sea. He decided to risk her not putting two and two together. Now, with Gina's rekindled interest, he feared she might uncover facts that would lead to his undoing. The need to eliminate Anna Northshield, and now perhaps Gina, would become a major focal point in Ted's thoughts.

"You have no right to burst in here and accuse me! Your husband nearly cost this bank a fortune and put my job on the line. In fact, Missus Donovan, if anyone should be mad, it should be me!"

"What? Are you crazy?"

"Your husband's little fuck-up cost me the presidency of this bank."

Gina stood, aghast. "You're putting a damn title, which you had no right to in the first place, ahead of my husband's life!"

"I'm not going to belabor the point. Now get out of here before I call security." He placed his hand on the telephone. "Well?"

"Okay, I'm going." Gina opened the door. "This isn't over! Someday! Somehow! I'll see you burn in hell!" She whirled and stalked from the office.

Moments later, Frances ran into the office. "Should I call the police?"

"No. No, let it go. But I don't take kindly to threats."

The last thing I need is the police snooping around here, Ted thought to himself.

Chapter 32

"Doc, this is Earl Collier. We have another dead body. Tom and I are on our way to Ted Jaffey's house. Mabel Harris found his body. He's been shot." Sheriff Collier pulled the squad car alongside Mabel's sedan, and the two men walked to the door, stomping wet snow from their boots.

"Thank God you're here, Earl...Tom." Mabel Harris opened the door and motioned them in. "The body is in the den on your left, just off the living room. I didn't touch anything except the phone in the kitchen when I called you."

"Good. When Doc Hadley shows up, let him in, please, and we could use a pot of coffee."

Mabel bustled out, happy to have something to occupy her time.

"The room looks like it was hit by a tornado and the safe's open," Earl noted.

"Yeah, maybe robbery. Jaffey surprised the guy, the guy shot him, panicked, and ran," Deputy Tom Fellows speculated.

"Call the lab boys and have them come dust for prints. In the meantime, I'll look around and see if I can find signs of forced entry. Let me know when Doc gets here."

A few minutes later, Tom Fellows located Earl in a back bedroom. "Doc's here and the coffee is on." The three men moved to the kitchen, where they joined Mabel at the round table, drinking coffee.

"I can't do much until your lab team is through," the coroner said, sipping his coffee. "I'll take the body to the office and run some tests and a preliminary autopsy. Notice those exit holes? Hollow-nose, if I was to make a guess."

"Mabel, when you got here, did you notice anything different or unusual?" the sheriff asked.

"No, other than the mess in the den and Mister Jaffey's body, of course."

"Did you use your key to get in or was the door unlocked?"

"I used my key. But I always do. Mister Jaffey is—was—so careful about locking up."

"So you don't know if the door was locked or not?"

"No, sir."

"Were the lights on in the den?"

"Yes, and in the kitchen."

They heard a knock on the front door.

"Must be the lab boys. Tom, have them start with the front door, then they can work on through the hall and den. And tell Robin to get his photos right away so Doc can get the body out of here. You and I are going to check with the neighbors, see if they saw or heard anything tonight. By the way, Mabel, what brought you to the house this evening?"

"Right in the middle of supper I couldn't remember if I had turned off the iron. I called and didn't get an answer. Mister Jaffey eats out sometimes, you know, being single and all. So I decided to drive over and take care of the iron myself. It wouldn't pay to have Mister Jaffey mad at me."

"You must have got here around seven? Your call to us was logged in at seven-oh-eight p.m. and you said you called us right away?"

Mabel nodded.

"You can go if you wish. I'll can call you if I need you again."

An hour later, the sheriff and deputy, having returned from canvassing the neighborhood, sat with the coroner in the living room. The body had been placed in a body bag and removed to the coroner's laboratory downtown.

"Okay, let's review what we have so far," Earl said, flipping open his notebook. "One, we know Jaffey was shot three times. Two, we don't have signs of forced entry."

"So what are you saying?" Tom asked.

"Well, nothing for sure, but the killer either came in to kill and tried to make it look like a robbery, or he was looking for something special and Jaffey walked in on him and was killed."

"If you didn't find forced entry, and based on what Mabel said about Jaffey being so careful about locking up, you have to believe Jaffey let the killer in. That means Jaffey knew the killer," Doc said.

"Not necessarily, but that's a damn good guess. But if the killer stuck a gun in Jaffey's face after he opened the door, then your theory goes out the window."

"It might help to know when he left work," Doc said.

"You're right. I'll call Frances Eldridge, Jaffey's secretary, and see if I can find out. I went to school with her."

"Fran? This is Earl Collier. I hate to bother you at home, but some of us guys are sitting around arguing about bankers' hours. It isn't nine to three or like that, is it? As an example, when did your boss go home tonight? I see. You just made me a dollar. Thanks, Frances.

"Jaffey left just before five. She knows because they walked to the parking lot together. That puts him home in fifteen or twenty minutes. I'd say we have the time of the killing as early as five fifteen, no later than seven, based on Mabel's call to our office."

"That makes it pretty easy for me to pin down the time of death." Doc Hadley smiled.

"Let's lock this place up and come back in the morning. I'll be up half the night doing my damn reports as it is. By the way, did you find the slugs?"

"Yes, nice little cluster in the wall panel by the bookcase. Looks like a thirty-eight," Tom said.

"Casings?"

"None."

"That's worth noting," Collier said. "Okay, guys, let's go."

Chapter 33

The Thursday following Ted Jaffey's murder, Sheriff Collier, Deputy Sheriff Fellows, the Coroner and Prosecuting Attorney David Sandburg sat in a small meeting room adjacent to the prosecutor's office.

"These are serious charges we're considering," Sandburg said.

"I know, Dave, but most of the pieces fit. First, Missus Donovan was heard arguing with Jaffey just a few days ago," Earl Collier said. "According to Jaffey's secretary, Missus Donovan threatened him, spoke of seeing him 'burn in hell.' Second, we have the letter from Missus Donovan saying she held him responsible for her husband's death. It was delivered to Jaffey's mailbox the morning after the murder."

"May I see the letter?" Sandburg asked. He glanced at the letter then read it aloud: "You are the vilest of men. You destroy a person as liquor destroys an alcoholic. You killed my husband drop by insidious drop, then tell me YOU are the victim of his poor judgement! I will not let the person who drove my husband to suicide go unpunished. I hold you responsible for breaking his spirit and causing him to take his life. The law and the courts may protect you, but you are not protected from me!"

"She even signed it," Sheriff Collier commented. "And she was there. A neighbor saw a car drive away from Jaffey's house around six o'clock that night. She described it as a dark sedan. Missus Donovan drove a dark blue 1960 Oldsmobile 98 sedan. We have a copy of a sales slip and a statement from the sales clerk, stating Flynn Donovan purchased a thirty-eight revolver less than a year ago. The clerk remembered the sale because Donovan asked for hollow points."

"Say why he was buying it?" Sandburg asked quietly.

"Something about prowlers. Said if the robber showed up at his house, he wanted to blow him away. I checked back, and we don't show any reports of robberies, prowlers, or even Peeping Toms around the time he bought the gun."

"Go on."

"Fingerprints in the den. The lab found Jaffey's, Mabel Harris's, and two clear prints of Missus Donovan's, one of her right thumb and one of her right index finger."

"How the hell did you get a match?"

"A stroke of luck, really. Gina Donovan sold real estate for a couple years in the early fifties. We were required to get fingerprints from all salesmen and saleswomen and run a criminal check on them for the State. We started keeping duplicates. I remembered, checked it out and she matched up."

"Good work. We have her at the scene, we have motivation, and we have what appears to be premeditation. This is a murder one."

"I feel sorry for old man Stern. He deserves better. God, his wife died not too long ago, his son-in-law commits suicide, now his daughter kills her husband's boss. What next?" Tom Fellows said, shaking his head.

"What's our next move?" Sheriff Collins asked.

"Bring her in for questioning. I'll prepare a warrant and get Judge Quinn's signature. Let me know when she's here. If she wants to call her attorney, fine," Sandburg said. "We're dealing with a leading citizen's family, so keep cool. By the way, did the lab confirm the slugs came from a thirty-eight?"

"Yes."

"We'd better get a search warrant to look for the gun. I want to show we did this one by the book, and more."

Chapter 34

The loss of Sarah and Flynn, and now Gina's arrest for the murder of Ted Jaffey, had created a void in his life, tears within the family fabric that, for now, seemed beyond repair. After fifty years of giving, sacrifice and altruistic acts, a backlash of selfish desire seized him. His fairness and unshaking integrity in business and personal transactions remained steadfast; his father's admonishment that people of wealth could not be trusted acted as the catalyst to be constantly vigilant of his stewardship of money. Loneliness and lack of a loving companion to share the personal and monetary rewards, once held so dear with Sarah, brought him to this self-serving turn of mind.

He missed Anna's counsel, her link to his childhood, her intuition and insight. Her absences during Flynn's suicide and now Gina's arrest created a void that no one else could fill.

Gina's attorney, Joseph Palmer, and Gina herself provided his only potential anchor. To burden either with his needs while each fought to save Gina from a first-degree murder charge was unthinkable.

As was his routine of late following Wesslin's retirement, George spent mornings at the bank, usually in his office on the executive floor. Available for senior loan committee meetings, visiting with long-time customers, or handling some public relations best suited his position as board chairman. He also enjoyed keeping in contact with the business community. All in all these activities gave him a sense of belonging.

It was also a time of change and challenge for the bank. Ed Gilbert had made the transition to president with relative ease. His replacement in the finance division was made through promotion and reassignment of responsibilities. The loss of Flynn and then Ted Jaffey within weeks of the other demanded major attention to the Loan Division's demoralized and divided staff, a key division to income producing and continued public trust. To make matters worse, First Commercial National Bank of Seattle, the largest bank in the state, opened a branch in Aurora. Reports showed deposit losses in excess of one million dollars and loan transfers approaching half a million. An aggressive, full-service bank, First Commercial showed signs of making additional inroads into Freeland's here- to-now exclusive banking territory. Together with Gilbert and other bank officers, concerted efforts were made in retaining customers. Meeting for the purpose of upgrading and training of the staff were held for all divisions emphasizing customer service. Several thousand dollars was earmarked for additional advertising in local and branch locations.

The many contacts Ed Gilbert had made through the years were rewarded with the hiring of a highly-qualified lending division vice-president. A native of the area and graduate of the State University in agriculture and finance, Robert Johnston had spent ten years associated in all aspects of commercial lending, especially in agriculturally related loans, with a major bank in California.

A young man of thirty-three, he exuded energy and optimism which soon invaded the loan division from managers to loan clerks. Within two months Johnston was well on the way to restoring confidence inside and outside the bank.

The cold storage, orchards, and shopping center had capable management teams demanding little of George's time or decision making. Now incorporated, he had begun to divest himself of ownership through stock gifts to various long-time loyal employees, his family, and endowments to local and regional institutions through the use of annual gifts, blind trusts, or other tax sheltering laws and regulations. He still lived comfortably with a personal net worth in excess of two million dollars.

Chapter 35

Elizabeth Ashbrook entered George Stern's life shortly after the Jaffey murder.

"I realize I'm being rather bold asking to see the Chairman, but I believe if you want things done you must seek the best person to help. In this case that person is you."

"I'm flattered, Miss Ashbrook."

"Mrs. My husband died recently. You may call me Elizabeth, or Beth, if you prefer."

Beth was a slender woman, forty-eight years old, with an engaging smile and dark, deep-set eyes. Auburn hair added to her youthful, athletic appearance, as did her well-proportioned figure. She spoke in a low, almost sultry voice.

George liked her immediately, admired her air of self-confidence and intelligence. "I'm sorry to hear of your loss. I lost my wife and know the pain. Now, Mrs. Ashbrook...Beth, how may I help you?"

She stood and removed her dark raincoat. The dark grey skirt and matching jacket with white ruffled blouse beneath presented a person of good taste. "My late husband and I owned a profitable motel and restaurant in Santa Barbara. I felt it too much for me to handle alone, so I sold it recently. I'm looking for an investment. Bonds, stocks, perhaps real estate, perhaps an orchard. I opened a modest checking and saving accounts with your bank this morning and asked to see you. It was not by accident, either. You have an enviable reputation in this town, Mister Stern."

George fidgeted uncomfortably, feeling a sensory, near sensual reaction to this lovely woman. "You flatter me. May I ask why you are in Aurora in the middle of winter and not in sunny California?"

"A reasonable question." She crossed her legs, revealing her trim calf to better advantage. "I was raised in the Midwest and enjoy the four seasons. However, severe winters and humid summers don't entice me. We traveled when we could and always liked Oregon and Washington, especially this part of Washington, and Aurora in particular. While not especially an outdoor person, I do like to walk and hike and go boating. This seemed a natural place to set down roots and start a new home."

George stared at her, not answering, taken again by a stirring inside he had not felt for some years. Beth met his look boldly, not flickering. A blush rose on George's face. He cleared his throat self-consciously and looked away.

"You mentioned investments," he said finally. "I could recommend a broker friend here or one in Seattle. As to real estate, I can introduce you to two or three reputable realtors in town. By the way, where are you staying?"

"I've taken rooms at the Aurora Arms temporarily, Apartment 405." George jotted down the address on his calendar pad. "Frankly, I'd hoped you might have time to show me the community and point out the better investment areas, best restaurants, that sort of thing."

"I'd be delighted. I know it's short notice, but would you be my guest at the country club this evening? It's our annual winter get-together, just dinner and a few drinks. Many of my friends and business associates will be there. It's a good way to break the ice."

"How very sweet of you to ask. Certainly, I'd love to go. Dress?"

"A bit formal. Some men wear evening tux, the women usually evening gowns or cocktail dresses. We try and make it a nice occasion. Shall we say six o'clock, then?"

"I'm looking forward to it, Mister Stern...George, if I may." She extended her hand and he shook it, slightly damp from his nervousness. He hoped she'd not noticed, but she had. She smiled inwardly. George held her coat, then walked her the short distance to the office door.

"Until six, then." She smiled and walked away, aware of George's admiring look as she went. He returned to his desk, a light sweat on his brow. *This is absurd!* he thought. *I'm acting like a damn school boy.* Strong, manly desires rose in his breast, and he did nothing to cure them. *There's life in the old boy yet,* he chortled. Six o'clock could not come too soon.

From the first evening with her, George moved to cementing an ongoing relationship. Beth had worn a knee-length white cocktail dress, a golden sash at her willowy waist, the skirt hugging her slender hips; a modest V-cut neckline with off-the-shoulder short sleeves displayed tawny skin of peaches and cream complexion. Immediately above the cleavage of her high, firm breasts hung a single two-carat diamond on a slender golden chain. Her hair was brushed to a high sheen, pulled tight on the sides and gathered with a small gold comb. Youthful in dress and appearance, most thought her to be nearer forty than fifty. A seductive perfume completed Beth's portrait of a woman.

Men hovered around her, envying George his good fortune; women were soon taken with her charm, while recognizing she represented a force to be reckoned with. Wives clung tighter to husbands, hands squeezed, promises whispered of later pleasures. So was the impact of Elizabeth Ashbrook's coming out in Aurora's social circle.

Chapter 36

Initially Gina had been granted bail, over the strong protests of Sandburg. Based on arguments by Palmer that Gina had no prior record, a daughter to raise, and a father willing to pledge a half-million dollars for her bond, bail was granted, providing Gina not leave the immediate area surrounding Aurora. Foolishly, she did so, having driven to the University some two hundred miles away when informed Shawn had been injured and was unconscious as a result of an automobile accident. While Shawn's injury was limited to a badly sprained ankle, bruises, and a mild concussion, Gina's actions violated her bail. The prosecuting attorney demanded and was successful in having her bond revoked despite Palmer's arguments that Gina's actions were those of a distraught mother and not without good cause. As a result, Gina had been returned to the county jail to await her scheduled trial date.

Her father's visits to jail each day gave her strength. Her sudden, unexpected return to prison had caused untold hardships on the household. Mike and Shawn continued their pursuit of degrees at school at the insistence of Gina and the encouragement of George. As for Margaret, now fifteen, she stayed with her grandfather at the Homeplace but found the arrangement unsatisfactory for many reasons. George arranged that a young, assistant operations officer and his wife move into Gina's house as caretakers. He also hired a woman to cook evening meals and help in maintaining the house since the operations officer's wife worked days as a receptionist at a local dentist's office. Margaret accepted the arrangement grudgingly, but soon made fast friends with the couple, appreciating a semblance of continuity in her life. She visited her mother daily, bringing news of school, family, and community. It was from Margaret that Gina learned of Beth.

"Your granddaughter tells me you've been seen in the company of an attractive younger woman, Papa." Gina cocked her head inquisitively across the table in the visitor's room.

"She's nearly fifty, if you consider that young. Yes, I've been with her occasionally, both business and pleasure. I'm giving her an opportunity to get acquainted. Do you find that upsetting?"

"Should I?" Gina countered.

"Surely you don't begrudge me a personal life."

"I thought you and Mama...it always seemed special somehow. I guess it never occurred to me there might be someone else someday."

George's last wish was to upset his daughter; he must calm her fears. "Beth and I are friends, dear, nothing more."

"My life is already in such an upheaval. I don't need you giving me something more to worry about."

"I don't understand."

"Oh, Papa, don't be so naive! A rich, handsome widower is the perfect target for any woman with selfish motivations. You're so trusting, so ignorant of life in some ways."

" I like Beth, and no, I haven't even considered marriage. But I will tell you this, young lady. You or no one else will stop me if that's what I decide to do!" Veins stood out at George's temples; his voice carried an anger Gina had not heard used against her even as a child. She was hurt and concerned.

"I'm sorry if I made you mad," Gina said, "but I'm not going to stand by and see you make a fool of yourself. Guard! I'm ready to go back now." Without another word or backward glance, she marched out, leaving her father sitting frustrated and uncertain.

On the ride home he thought of Beth and Sarah. He would never stop loving Sarah—the years together, the trials and joys. The birth of the Gina, the many secret, wonderful moments they had shared together. They had talked about this very possibility, should either die. She had put her hand on his face. "Darling, I always want you to be happy. You'll need someone to take care of you, hold you, and listen to you. If I'm not here and someone else comes along—well, that's life, and death."

Chapter 37

Feeling the Freeland Bank situation resolved for the present, George had broken his routine of daily visits to his office, spending more and more time with Joseph Palmer, Gina's attorney, his other business interests, and his newfound companion. One evening, George and Beth arrived at the Homeplace shortly past seven. Following a light supper, they sat in the matching chairs flanking the fireplace, the warmth of an after-dinner coffee and the fire making them relaxed and comfortable.

"You still don't know me very well, my dear. For you to be concerned about these rumors that I am selling my shares or have agreed to a merger with an out-of-state bank are simply not true. George Stern does not abandon his friends or this community. I nurtured that bank from the day it opened, risked a quarter-million dollars of my own money when that was a king's ransom. I'm not a quitter."

"Nor am I suggesting you are." She put her cup down and came to curl at his feet. She wore dark slacks, a light, pale blue jersey pullover and slippers that she now kicked off, wiggling her toes and pushing her feet toward the fire. Head against his knee, she felt secure in the knowledge that he was hers. He ran his fingers lightly across the nape of her neck, gathering strands of hair between his fingers and letting them fall across her shoulders. She wondered if this might be the night that he'd ask her to his bed. Once there, she knew he would be hers—body, soul and fortune. But she was patient, although both patience and bank accounts were getting thin. Her lies of being financially secure, and especially of the death of a husband, had opened doors to opportunity; now they may stand in the way of

George becoming more involved in the relationship. *His old-fashioned morals may yet prove my downfall,* Beth worried.

"Any news of Gina's trial date?" she asked.

"Next month is Palmer's best guess."

"I'd like to meet Gina."

"You will, when this is over. Right now you're not one of her favorite people."

"Because she sees me taking away from Sarah's memory?" She almost said "taking Sarah's place as your wife," but caught herself.

"Yes, but time will change that. She'll grow to love you as I do."

She rose and eased herself into his lap, arms around his neck. "Did I just hear you mention 'love' and me in the same breath?" She said it in an off-handed, almost teasing way.

"You did, and I am starting to fall in love with you, you wanton woman." He drew her to him, kissing her tenderly.

She pressed against him, responding. Nice," she whispered in his ear, "hmm...very nice."

He drew back slightly, tracing her lips and cheek with his forefinger. "You are truly lovely. I'm a lucky man to have found you."

If you only knew who found whom, she laughed inwardly. *A near admission of love; I'm winning!*

"This could go on and on, but I have a busy day tomorrow, so it's time to take you home."

She pressed against him, face upturned, eyes nearly closed. "One more kiss?"

He obliged, feeling a strong urge within his groin. It was with supreme effort that he released her. *Not in this house, not in Sarah's house, not yet.* He helped her up, into her warm jacket and to the car, holding her tightly against the late winter chill. She knew her scheme was coming to fruition. She needed a month, maybe two. Right after Gina's trial would be perfect. She sat close to him on the ride home, talking little, letting the presence of her body with her hand resting casually on his leg be her messenger.

Chapter 38

"Papa, I'm glad you came," Gina said. "I've missed your visits."

They talked of Margaret and her visits, Joe's latest efforts preparing for the trial, Shawn's and Mike's visit home the previous weekend, the weather, everything but the subject both knew was foremost on the other's mind.

Finally Gina broke the ice. "Are you still seeing Mrs. Ashbrook?"

"Yes."

"Margaret tells me there is talk of marriage."

"Not from me. People like to spread rumors, as you well know." He waited, letting Gina set the direction.

"Will you marry her someday?"

"Perhaps, if she'd have me."

"'Have you,' dear fool? You're ripe for the picking." Her voice was low and controlled, though anger showed in her eyes and clenched jaw. She sat tense and upright, her fists in two tight balls, knuckles white. George showed a placid countenance that fueled Gina's anger the more, but was also determined he would not to be drawn into another discussion about Beth. Gina was acting irrational, as she had against Ted Jaffey, without basis of fact—woman's intuition, she'd probably say—and in Jaffey's case it had landed her in jail. Would she not learn to curb her outbursts?

"Well, say something! Convince me I'm wrong!"

George continued his silence, merely shaking his head, waiting.

"Your silence says it all. You don't care how I feel about this, do you! I could rot in this goddamned jail while you run around with your mistress. My mother and your family must be worth this to you!" She formed a zero with her thumb and first finger.

"If you weren't across that table and a guard watching, I'd give you a spanking for acting so childish. There isn't a day goes by I don't think of your mother. There isn't a day, or night, that I don't pray for you, worry for you, yes, cry for you. If I could trade places with you now, I'd do so without a moment's hesitation. I love you, daughter, perhaps more than you can ever know; but I will tell you this also, you, or no one else, will tell me how to run my personal life. As for Beth—yes, I hope to marry her after you're freed. If you choose to dislike her, or me, for it, I'm sorry."

"If you meant all those platitudes, you wouldn't marry her. But if you do, I don't want to be a part of your life anymore!"

"Now my daughter is threatening me." He shook his head sadly. "They can add blackmail to your list of crimes." His promise to avoid a fight had burst to a full-blown war.

"Papa! You think I murdered Ted?"

"God, no! A cruel remark made in anger. I'm sorry, truly sorry."

The combatants paused, gathering strength, collecting thoughts. George broke the silence. "I have no intention of marrying Beth or even asking her until this mess is over. Let's pull together for now and iron out this Beth situation later."

The smoldering anger cooled in Gina. Deep down she knew she needed her father now more than ever, not his money—though that helped—but his love and strength. The Ashbrook affair could be dealt with in its own time. George left the jail, drained. He loved Beth, he knew, but he loved his daughter more. Engagements and marriage would have to wait.

Chapter 39

The newspaper article began:

> *Flanked by the tall, erect, and distinguished presence of her father, George Stern, and her attorney, Joseph Palmer, Gina Marie (Stern) Donovan appeared more petite than usual when she appeared in court today. Her carriage, her firm jaw, and the challenge in her eyes revealed an inner strength and resolve. The unexpected arrest some months ago of one of Aurora's leading family members on first degree murder charges has galvanized the attention of this quiet, rural community.*
>
> *David Sandburg, the young, energetic prosecuting attorney, has indicated a conviction of Mrs. Donovan is, in his words, "air tight."*

The trial was in its second day, a jury selected with each side having made its opening remarks.

"Now, Miss Eldridge, tell us exactly what happened the day Missus Donovan came to Mister Jaffey's office," David Sandburg asked.

Frances sat with eyes downcast for the moment. "She came by my desk and demanded to see Mister Jaffey. I told her he was busy and couldn't be disturbed, but she insisted. Then Mister Jaffey came out. They both went into his office and had a big argument."

"Objection," Joseph Palmer's voice thundered across the room. "Speculation on the part of the witness." Bulky, slow-moving Palmer, whose voice and mannerisms commanded the stage on which he practiced his theatrics, settled back in his chair.

"Miss Eldridge," Judge Quinn asked, "was the office door open or closed?"

"Closed, Your Honor, but later Mister Jaffey told me she threatened him."

"Objection! Hearsay...please, Your Honor."

"Sustained. The testimony regarding what Mister Jaffey said will be stricken. Jury is instructed to disregard that portion of the witness's remark."

"Would you say they were talking in loud tones?" Sandburg asked.

"Yes, well, she was...I couldn't hear him."

"You couldn't hear what was being said in the office?"

"No, not exactly."

"But later, outside the office, what did Missus Donovan say?"

"As she left, she said, 'This isn't over, I'll see you burn in hell first!'"

The audience in the crowded courtroom whispered and mumbled, then grew silent.

"Those are her exact words? This is important."

"'I'll see you burn in hell,' is what she said."

"And you took that to mean...?"

"Objection! Calls for conclusion by the witness."

"Sustained."

"Your witness," Sandburg said.

Joseph Palmer approached the stand and put his hand on the witness box rail. "Frances Eldridge," he said reflectively. "You Bob and Edith's daughter?"

"Yes, sir."

"How long had you been Mister Jaffey's secretary?"

"About five years, five years this coming June."

"Was he a good boss, easy to work for?"

"He...."

"Objection. Mister Palmer's questions have nothing to do with this case."

"I think I can show a connection if I may ask a few more questions,

Your Honor."

"Continue, but please make your point."

"Thank you. Was Ted Jaffey a good boss? Was he easy to work for?"

"Well, he had his days, but yes, he was good to me the majority of the time."

"And you were loyal to him?"

"Yes."

"Why is it you've never married? You're an attractive young lady."

"Objection! This line of questioning is totally irrelevant."

"I tend to agree. Make your point, Mister Palmer," the judge said.

"An unmarried, attractive young woman working for a handsome, successful banker. Did you have more than a business relationship with your employer? Did you love him?"

"Objection!"

"Sustained."

"How do you feel about Missus Donovan?"

"I don't even know her except to say 'hello.'"

"Then you have no opinion of her one way or the other?"

"I feel sorry for her, but—"

"How did you feel the day she called you," Palmer checked his notes quickly, "'a little piece of fluff'?"

Frances's face reddened slightly. "I-I—"

"It made you mad, didn't it? A woman comes into your office, calls you a 'piece of fluff'—then makes derogatory remarks about the man you love?"

"Objection!"

"I have no further questions." Palmer sat down and whispered to Gina, "That may make a dent in her credibility. We can only wait and see."

Sandburg stood. "Just one more question, Miss Eldridge, did you love Mr. Jaffey?"

"No!"

"Thank you."

The remainder of the morning was devoted to Dr. Hadley's

testimony concerning cause of death—three .38 caliber hollow-nosed slugs through the chest—and his final conclusion that death occurred sometime between five p.m. and seven p.m.

"Doctor, when did you first see the body—not perform the autopsy, but physically view the body?" Palmer asked.

"According to my notes, seven thirty-four p.m. the night of the murder."

"I see. From that examination, what can you tell us about the body?"

"The deceased was laying face-down...."

"I'm sorry, Doctor, perhaps I misstated my question. Let me be more direct. You say he died between five and seven p.m. Is your conclusion based on knowledge of when he left work and when Mabel Harris discovered the body at approximately seven o'clock?"

"Yes."

"Can you tell us, based on your examinations at the house and in your lab, whether death occurred more closely to seven or to five o'clock?"

"Closer to five o'clock, in all probability."

"Based on?"

"Temperature of the body, slight rigor mortis of the fingers, lack of leakage from the wounds."

"Any discoveries during the autopsy that altered your initial impressions?"

"No."

"Would it be more reasonable for your report to read the probable time of death to be between five and five thirty?"

"I can't be that precise."

"Five and six o'clock?"

"I could live with that."

"So, to restate, in your opinion, death most likely occurred sometime between five and six o'clock?"

"Yes, in all probability."

"Thank you. Thank you very much." Palmer returned to his chair at the counsel table.

"That sounded encouraging, Mister Palmer. I was still in the Swiftwater Canyon!" Gina whispered.

"I know, but we can't prove you were there. We have no witnesses except your mysterious young lady in the phantom sports car."

"I hope we find her soon."

"Where do we begin? You've given us so little to go on. No make or year—you're not even sure it was a Washington State plate."

"I wish I'd paid more attention," Gina said sadly. "But I couldn't guess it would be my alibi to a murder charge."

Chapter 40

The afternoon testimony proved more damaging.

"In your expert opinion, whose fingerprints are displayed in the Exhibits J and K?"

"The defendant's, Missus Gina Donovan."

"And you found them where?"

"On the doorjamb in the hallway by the den."

"Thank you. Your witness, Mister Palmer."

"Mister Barker, did you find any other prints of my client at the scene?"

"No."

"How do you account for that?"

"Objection. Conjecture on the part of the witness."

"Sustained."

"Did you find Missus Donovan's prints on the drawers? The desk? The safe? In fact, did you find them anywhere other than on the wooden doorjamb in the hallway?"

"No, sir."

"With so many scientific advances today, is there a method whereby one can determine when the prints were placed there?"

"Do you mean can I say a certain day or week?"

"Yes."

"No. While prints do age—as an example, a fresh print is greasier—I can't pin an older print's age to exact days or weeks."

"Now you also found prints of Mister Jaffey?"

"Yes."

"Mabel Harris?"

"Yes."

"Anyone else?"

"No."

"But you said in your report you found smudged prints?"

"Yes, I did."

"What does that indicate?"

"Objection!"

"Denied. This is within the realm of witness's field as I view it," Judge Quinn ruled.

Barker continued, "Well, it can mean many things."

"Such as? Give us some examples."

"Someone puts their prints over existing prints. He or she doesn't press hard enough to leave a print. He or she moves or rubs their fingers across a surface and erases the good prints. The type of surface may not accept a print, things of that nature."

"How about someone wearing gloves? Wouldn't that leave smudged prints?"

"There are no prints from gloves."

"I understand. But gloves can smudge prints?"

"Oh, yes."

"Then it's possible someone else could have been in the room?"

"It's possible."

"Thank you, that will be all."

"Just a moment, Mister Barker," said Sandburg. "Smudged prints may indicate the existence of prior prints, am I correct?"

"Yes."

"So it's possible prints left by Missus Donovan in other parts of the house could be among those smudged?"

"It's possible, yes."

"How many prints of Mister Jaffey and Missus Harris did you find in the den or its entrance?"

"My records show two of Mister Jaffey's on the safe door and a drinking glass on the desk. The two of Missus Harris's were on the glass-topped desk of a small table in the corner of the den in addition to several of both Jaffey and Missus Harris in and around the kitchen area."

"So you found equal numbers of prints for Jaffey, Harris, and Donovan in and around the den?"

"Correct."

"It would follow that the erased prints, in all probability, occurred after any original prints were placed there?"

"Objection! This is leading. Mister Barker has already stated smudged prints are not exclusive of an 'overlay,' so to speak," Palmer interrupted.

"I'll allow the question, providing Mister Sandburg rephrases the question and Mister Barker makes the explanation clear to all of us," the judge said.

"Just one moment." Palmer was on his feet. "We haven't established when Missus Donovan was there; therefore, we can't know she smeared the prints. It calls for supposition and conclusions, not based on established facts. I ask the last question and answer be stricken."

"I concur. Strike. Jury is advised to ignore the question."

Sandburg plunged on, "Despite your early testimony regarding the 'aging' of fingerprints, can you say with any certainty how recently Missus Donovan had been in Jaffey's house?"

"Based on the freshness of the oil content, I would say sometime within twenty-four hours of the decease's death."

"Thank you. That will be all."

"One clarifying question, if I may?" asked Palmer. "Mister Barker, does lack of finding other prints preclude someone else having been in the room? Or being the one who smudged the prints?"

"No, I would think not."

"Thank you."

Chapter 41

Nearing the conclusion of the two-week trial, Joe Palmer, George, and Gina sat in a small room in the courthouse reviewing the case.

"Taking each item separately—as an example, the neighbor who saw a car, the fact Flynn purchased a thirty-eight revolver—does not hold as good, substantial evidence. In fact, most all the evidence is circumstantial. But if one adds each of the events together, the question of reasonable doubt becomes less and less likely."

"But I didn't do it!"

"You know that, your father and I know that, but the jury must look at the evidence as presented—and some that isn't."

"Meaning?"

"Jurors are honest people. However, they often remember facts they are told not to remember or consider. The memory is there, lurking in the back of the juror's mind. Frances Eldridge's comment that you threatened to kill Ted is implanted. The judge told the jury to ignore it, and each will to the best of his ability. But if you're a juror and you're on the fence, isn't that statement about you wanting to kill him going to come back? Perhaps tip the scale?"

Gina cringed. "You frighten me."

"I'm sorry, I don't mean to, but we must face facts. Let's talk about whether or not to put you on the stand."

"You mean there could be a reason not to?" George asked, surprise in his question.

"Yes. Once she testifies, she's open to Sandburg's attacks."

"I thought he could only address questions pertaining to areas you raise," Gina said.

"That's how it's supposed to work. But almost anything I say—

or certainly you say—opens the floodgates. You're not going to convince a jury of your innocence if I ask, 'Did you ever kill anyone?' and you say 'No,' and I dismiss you. Your honesty and innocence is going to be more clearly defined by how you handle both my questions and Sandburg's."

"I'll do my best."

"I know you will."

Chapter 42

The next day Gina sat alert and poised in the witness chair. She wore a handsome pale blue wool suit, a starched white blouse, collar high and modest. Her dark stockings and blue pumps gave her an appearance of grace and charm, of a genteel upbringing. Her salt-and-pepper hair, clean and shining, framed the delicately chiseled features of her face.

Joseph Palmer walked slowly to the witness box. "Gina, I want you to look at the jury when you answer my question. Did you kill Theodore Jaffey?"

She met the stares of the jurors with openness and frankness, not wavering under their studied gaze. "No. I did not."

"Gina, are you aware your husband purchased a thirty-eight revolver approximately a year ago?"

"No. Well, yes, but not until we were told of it a few days ago."

"I see." Joe Palmer picked up a sales slip and handed it to Gina. "Are you familiar with Al's Gun Shop?"

"I know of it, yes."

"Have you ever been in the store?"

"No."

"Purchased a gun or shells from that store or any other store?"

"No."

"Your husband didn't discuss buying a revolver either before or after its purchase?"

"We never talked about it. I didn't know Flynn owned a gun."

"How do you personally feel about guns?"

"I don't like them...they bother me."

"Why?"

"Years ago, when I was a little girl, I went hunting with my father. He shot a deer, and I cried. I never went hunting again."

"Have you ever held a gun? Shot a gun of any kind?"

"No, never."

"The time of Mr. Jaffey's death has been established between the hours of five and six o'clock the evening of January 24. Please tell the court where you were at that time."

"I was in my car in Swiftwater Canyon, driving toward Aurora."

"What were the road conditions? The weather?"

"The roadway was extremely icy. Often I drove as slowly as twenty-five miles an hour. It was snowing intermittently."

"At approximately what time did you arrive in Aurora?"

"About seven."

"Did you go directly home?"

"No."

"Tell us, where did you go?"

"I went to Ted Jaffey's home."

"Again, what time was that?"

"Just before seven. I remembered thinking I was late in picking up my daughter from her singing lesson."

"Why did you go to see Mister Jaffey?"

"To retrieve the letter I had foolishly mailed him."

"Did you have any other purpose in mind?"

"No. Well, perhaps to apologize for the letter."

"But no other reason?"

"No."

"In your own words, tell us what happened when you arrived at the Jaffey house. Take your time, be sure of your facts." Palmer walked to a spot in front of the jury box, forcing Gina to look in his direction as she answered.

"I parked my car and walked across the street to his front door and knocked. The door was apparently ajar, because my knocking caused the door to push open. I called his name a few times, but got no answer. Then...."

"Excuse me, what made you think Mister Jaffey was home?"

"Lights were on in the kitchen and down the hallway. I could see them behind the drawn drapes. And I could see tire tracks into the garage."

"Thank you, please continue," Palmer said.

"I pushed the door open and walked down the entry hallway, again calling his name. I thought he might be in his bedroom. When I got to the living room, I called once more and received no answer. The den is just off the living room, and that's when I saw him lying dead on the floor."

"To save the prosecutor time in cross-examination, how did you know he was dead?"

"The blood...the way his back was blown apart is the best way I can describe it. It was ghastly!"

"I'm sure it was. What else did you see?"

"The room was a mess. Papers, books, desk drawers thrown around. Furniture turned over. Oh, yes, the wall safe was open."

"What did you do then?"

"I ran outside and drove home."

"What time was that again?"

" A few minutes after seven o'clock."

"Can you estimate how long you were in the house?"

"Three minutes, five at the most."

"One last question. Did you kill Theodore Jaffey?"

"Again, I say no. No, I did not kill Ted Jaffey."

"Thank you, Gina." Palmer turned to David Sandburg. "Your witness."

"Missus Donovan, I'd like to review portions of your testimony, if I may." He walked toward her and stood to one side of her chair. "You say you were in Swiftwater Canyon when Mister Jaffey was killed?"

"Yes."

"Do you have any witnesses who could prove that?"

"Yes and no."

"Either you do or you don't. I see no witness listed to confirm on your story."

"If I could be allowed to explain?"

"Please do."

"As I said, the roadway was very dangerous. Coming around a curve, a large truck nearly forced me into the ditch. It frightened me. Fortunately, there was a turnout nearby, so I pulled in and got out of my car to get some fresh air. That's when a young lady in a sports car stopped to see if I needed assistance. I assured her I was all right and she drove away."

"I see. You can't describe the driver other than she was young and driving a fancy sports car. That's your alibi?"

"That, and I know I'm telling the truth."

"How would you describe your feelings toward Mister Jaffey?"

"Objection."

"On what grounds, Mister Palmer?" Judge Quinn asked brusquely.

"On the grounds it doesn't constitute proper cross-examination. My client did not express or discuss her relationship with Mister Jaffey in any way during her testimony."

"Mister Sandburg, the ball is in your court." The judge sat back, waiting.

"I have precedent. In 'Wilcox versus Rodale,' California, nineteen fifty-seven, the Supreme Court held: 'The admittance of any hearsay evidence in the form of memoranda, letters, notes, or other handwritten documents subsequently established to be written by a defendant may be considered for purposes in cross-examination as if such content had been spoken by said defendant in oral testimony.' I submit the letter Missus Donovan wrote to Mister Jaffey has been properly submitted to the court during previous testimony. Therefore, based on the case just cited, my question regarding her feelings toward Mister Jaffey is proper."

"Exception!"

"Exception noted."

"I would point out also that Missus Donovan stated a few minutes ago, when asked by her own counsel why she went to Jaffey's house, quote, 'To retrieve the letter I had foolishly mailed him,' end of quote. Note she said 'the' letter, not 'a' letter. I submit 'the' letter she was talking about was the letter found in Jaffey's mailbox the next day, and which was subsequently admitted as our Exhibit M."

"Based on the California case and prior testimony, I will allow the question."

"Thank you, Your Honor."

"Would the clerk read back the question, please?"

The clerk scanned her notes, then read, "How would you describe your feelings toward Mister Jaffey?"

"You may answer, Missus Donovan," Judge Quinn said.

"I didn't like him."

"Isn't that statement rather mild, considering you wished to see him 'burned in hell,' and 'he would have to answer to you'? I submit you hated him. Hated him enough to kill him!"

"Objection! That is for summary, not cross."

"Let's keep the theatrics down, Mr. Sandburg."

"Yes, Your Honor."

"Continue."

"Would you wish to reconsider your last statement, Missus Donovan?"

"I disliked him intensely. Is that better?" A touch of anger was revealed in Gina's tone.

"You blame him for your husband's suicide?"

"I believe he drove him to suicide, yes."

"Then Mister Jaffey got what was coming to him?"

"Objection!"

"Sustained."

"Why did you park across the street and not in Mister Jaffey's driveway?"

"I don't know. It was icy, and I didn't want to get stuck, I suppose."

"Is your car equipped with snow tires?"

"Yes."

"You stated earlier you had driven over one hundred miles on dangerous highways, a goodly portion in Swiftwater Canyon, one of the most hazardous roads in this state, then ask us to believe you feared parking in a driveway? Come, Missus Donovan, do you take us for fools?"

"Your Honor! Mister Sandburg is casting aspersions upon my client and this court!"

"Mister Sandburg, I agree—that last remark was uncalled for."

"I apologize, Your Honor, and to you, Missus Donovan. The fact remains, you did park away from his house, not in the driveway."

"Yes."

"Now, when you knocked and the door opened, why did you go in?"

"I told you, to see Mister Jaffey and get my letter."

"If Mister Jaffey had not been present and you had found the letter, would you have taken it and left undetected?"

"Objection. Calls for speculation on the part of the witness."

"Sustained."

"Let me restate. Had you seen the letter, what might you have done?"

"Objection! Calls for supposition and possible self-incrimination."

"Sustained. Perhaps you should steer your boat off these rocky shoals, Mister Sandburg."

The audience laughed; even Gina managed a small grin.

"When you discovered Mister Jaffey's body, I believe you said, 'I ran to the car and drove home'—something to that effect. Is my statement basically correct?"

"Yes."

"You didn't call the police from Jaffey's house?"

"No."

"Perhaps when you got home?"

"No."

"Did you call your father or a close friend?"

"No."

"Did you tell your daughter what you had discovered?"

"I didn't, no."

"Tell me, Missus Donovan, why didn't you telephone or tell someone what had happened?"

"I don't know. I—I suppose I should have. I was afraid. But I didn't kill him! I didn't! I didn't! I'm telling the truth." Gina's resolve had been breached. She sat weeping.

Joe Palmer lumbered to her side, offering a handful of tissue.

"Would you like a few minutes?" Judge Quinn asked.

"No...thanks, Your Honor, I'll be all right." Gina wiped away her tears and sat erect, determination again showing in her posture.

"Had you ever been in the Jaffey home before the night you...before the night he died?" Sandburg resumed his questioning.

"Yes, a few times."

"Then you had knowledge of his wall safe? Its location?"

"No. I didn't know about a safe."

"A wall safe would be a good place to store worthwhile items, wouldn't you agree?"

"I would think so, yes."

"Perhaps you thought your letter was in the safe and killed him to get it!"

"No!" Then, more calmly, "No, I repeat, I did not kill Ted Jaffey."

"To review briefly, earlier testimony suggests no signs of forced entry. Missus Harris indicates the front door appeared locked when she arrived. You do admit to going to Ted Jaffey's home?"

"Yes."

"The purpose, according to you, to retrieve the letter you wrote to him, our Exhibit M?"

"Yes."

"And when you got there you believed him to be home because you saw lights on in the house and tire tracks in the drive, correct?"

"Yes, that's correct."

"Thank you. No more questions."

"Redirect, Mister Palmer?" Judge Quinn asked.

"Yes, thank you." Palmer resumed his spot in front of the jury box.

"You arrived at the deceased's home at seven?"

"Yes."

"Not five o'clock or even six o'clock?"

"No, sir."

"And he was dead when you arrived?"
"Yes."
"Thank you, Gina, I have no more questions."
"You may step down" Judge Quinn said, "Would both attorneys please approach the bench? Gentlemen, it is nearly noon. Do we have any more business or can we go to summary this afternoon?"
"I'm satisfied," Sandburg said.
"I want to call her daughter to support Missus Donovan's contention she arrived home past seven."
"Anyone else?"
"No."
"Good. You put her daughter on at one thirty, and then we'll go to summary. With luck, I can charge the jury this afternoon. Thank you, gentlemen." He raised his gavel. "Court dismissed. Reconvene at one thirty this afternoon. Jury is again admonished not to discuss the case among themselves or with anyone."

Chapter 43

Following Margaret's testimony sustaining her mother's testimony of that morning, the defense rested its case. After a short recess, David Sandburg addressed the jury with an opening statement as to the importance of each juror's role in meting out fair justice, then launched into his justification for a first-degree murder charge.

"I believe we have the elements necessary to our case, relating to motive and opportunity. We have irrefutable proof the defendant was at the scene of the crime, evidenced by her fingerprints and her own admission. Ask yourself, would an innocent person upon finding a dead body not call the police or tell a family member? Missus Donovan made no attempt to tell anyone. I consider that oversight equal to an admission of guilt! Based on testimony from witnesses, and a letter in her own handwriting, defendant threatened Mister Jaffey's life. While she now claims no knowledge of a thirty-eight-caliber pistol and hollow-point bullets, we know her late husband purchased these items within the last twelve months. I submit she shot the deceased, drove to a secluded spot, disposed of the weapon and bullets, waited a reasonable time, and drove home.

"I further submit defendant went to Mister Jaffey's home with the sole intention of killing him. The attempt to make it appear a robbery had occurred or was the motivation for being in the house fails, since the rest of the premises were undisturbed. Barring that scenario, the room could have been ransacked in her desperate attempt to find the letter in which she threatened his life.

"There was no sign of forced entry. That would lead one to believe Mister Jaffey admitted the killer of his own free will—knew who his killer was. I can draw two simple conclusions as to how entrance was obtained. Either Missus Donovan followed Mister Jaffey home and into the house when he opened the garage door, or she merely knocked at the door and was invited in.

"She has no alibi for the time in question. Her story of a phantom lady in a phantom car has no substantiation. Despite efforts by defense—and yes, by the county sheriff's department—no 'witness' has come forward. Lastly, we have a neighbor's testimony swearing she heard and saw a car of the general size and color of Missus Donovan's nineteen-sixty Oldsmobile speed away from the Jaffey house at approximately six o'clock the night of the murder.

"So we have motive—Missus Donovan's obsession that Jaffey had a major role in causing her husband's suicide. Couple that with verbal and written threats, and we have strong justification to support a murder charge. Means? Her husband's revolver. Opportunity? She was in the house the evening of the murder. Alibi? Unsubstantiated and unsupported. Defense witnesses? None.   "Based on good, logical reasoning and deduction, we have a solid case. I ask the jury to find Missus Gina Marie Donovan guilty of the premeditated murder of Theodore Jaffey. I ask you to convict her of murder in the first degree."

The jury and audience had listened carefully to Sandburg's remarks. They now relaxed, shifting in their seats, adjusting clothing. A few in the audience exchanged whispered remarks. Judge Quinn waited a few moments before bringing the court back to order.

"Mister Palmer, are you ready for the defense?"

"Yes, Your Honor. Ladies and gentlemen of the jury, the prosecutor's entire case is built on circumstantial evidence. Aside from the fact that he can place my client in Mister Jaffey's home—a fact Missus Donovan readily admits to—his case is built on a shaky foundation of supposition, guesswork, and wishful thinking.

"Let's review the prosecutor's case point by point. Wishing to see someone 'burn in hell' hardly constitutes a life-threatening statement. I dare say half of us in this room are accused of wrongdoing and condemned to hell every Sunday from the pulpits of the churches in our fair city.

"The claim to Missus Donovan having used her husband's revolver? She has stated in sworn testimony she had no knowledge of the gun. A search of her home produced no weapon. How can you place the smoking gun in her hand when there is no gun?

"Let's touch briefly on the killing itself. 'Three bullets through the chest in a nice, tight cluster.' Hardly the work of a woman totally unfamiliar with guns.

"Mister Sandburg rejects my client's alibi of the woman in Swiftwater Canyon as a lie. If she had truly planned to kill Mister Jaffey, would she not have established a more convincing story? Be seen in public, talked with friends, been highly visible just before and just after the crime? The truth is, no one saw her or talked to her from noon until she arrived home shortly after seven. Hardly the actions of someone needing or attempting to establish an alibi.

"Further, if she had intended to kill Jaffey, why call attention to herself by mailing a potentially incriminating letter to her victim a day or two before the crime was to be committed?

"The prosecutor makes much of Missus Donovan not calling the police upon discovering Jaffey's body. Who can say how any one of us would have reacted, knowing you would be a potential suspect in the case? She admits she may have erred. We have all been in situations where hindsight dictates. Grant her the right to be human to make a mistake in judgement.

"The neighbor who saw my client's car at the scene? Her description could fit several makes and models. We are accused of producing a phantom sports car. I suggest the prosecutor has produced a phantom case.

"Above all, we must evaluate Missus Donovan. A native of our community, a member of the valley's leading family, educated, and active in charities, church, and school, the mother of two fine sons and a talented daughter. This is hardly the profile of a murderess. You watched her on the stand, you saw and heard the honesty and sincerity in her words, her tone, and her eyes.

"Don't allow an innocent person to be crucified on the cross of circumstantial evidence. I know my client is innocent, and I trust in your wisdom as ladies and gentlemen of integrity and high standards, you, too, believe Gina to be innocent. In the name of justice, find her not guilty! Thank you."

Palmer walked back to the defense table as reporters and photographers crowded toward the railing. He swaggered a bit, enjoying the limelight.

"You people!" Judge Quinn shouted, pounding his gavel. "You're stretching the meaning of freedom of the press beyond reasonable bounds. Sit down!" The room became silent; only a muffled cough was heard. "That's better." Judge Quinn studied his notes carefully, jotting remarks in the margins. "Any additional comments, gentlemen?"

"No, Your Honor," each answered

"Thank you. We will take a brief ten-minute recess, after which I will charge the jury."

"All rise!"

The jury retired to the anteroom. The audience talked among themselves, many deciding to leave. Gina noticed Beth was there, as she had been throughout the trial, sitting next to George, a picture of loyal devotion.

George moved inside the railing, hugged Gina, shook Joe's hand. "I've been watching the jury while both you and Sandburg spoke. I can't read them one way or the other."

"Don't try. I gave that up a long time ago."

"Do you have a feeling about how it went? I thought you countered Sandburg's point very well," Gina said.

"I don't wish to speculate. You did splendidly this morning and certainly didn't hurt our case."

"How long will it take to get a verdict?"

"I've seen decisions so fast the jury chairs don't get cold. Others take days or weeks."

"God, I thought the waiting for the trial—and the trial itself—was hell. Now you tell me it could be days before they decide!"

"They have a lot to consider. I'm guessing, but unless they come to a quick decision, it will take two to three days."

Chapter 44

It was late evening of the third day of deliberation when the court reconvened. After all were seated, the judge asked the foreman for the verdict.

"We the jury find the defendant guilty of first-degree murder."

"So say you all?" the judge asked.

"Yes," they responded.

"Demand a polling of the jury!" Palmer said.

"You will answer 'guilty' or 'not guilty' as your name is read," the judge said.

Each responded 'guilty,' some looking at Gina, others not. As for Gina, she collapsed forward, head on her arms, her small frame convulsing with sobs she could not control. George knelt on the floor beside her, a look of disbelief on his face. He looked older than his sixty-eight years.

"Joe, I can't believe this!"

"I'm sorry, George. I sure as hell tried."

"What now?"

"Automatic appeal. Jesus!" He sat down heavily in a chair nearby.

A small gathering in the back of the courtroom filed out, the reporters anxious to write the story.

Through her tears and shock, Gina heard Judge Quinn dismiss the jury with his thanks, then request that Gina be removed from the courtroom and returned to her cell. She felt the gentle tug on her sleeve by the deputy. "Come, Missus Donovan, please."

Gina clutched George's arms. "Oh, Papa, what will happen to Margaret and the boys? This is a nightmare—it can't be real!"

"Please, Missus Donovan," the deputy said softly.

"Go with him, dear. I'll visit with Joe and get back to you tomorrow."

Gina left, leaning against the deputy for support. Her head was down, body bent forward at the shoulders. For the first time since her ordeal began, Gina Donovan's spirit was broken.

Chapter 45

Gina sat on the bed staring at a patch of sunlight that came through a high window in her cell. Thoughts hammered in her brain. From articles she had read and reread in the morning papers, it appeared a hung jury had been considered at one time. Several newspapers had quoted the jury foreman:

> *"Our biggest difficulty came when considering each piece of evidence by itself and then the evidence overall. We could provide reasons to find her innocent in a single circumstance, but when grouped together, the likelihood of all the happenings being unrelated just didn't hold up. It's too bad, she seems like a nice lady.*
>
> *"We almost had a hung jury. One juror initially held out. When he said he'd change his vote since the eleven others had agreed, we all, to a person, insisted he could be right, the rest wrong. It was then that I knew the jury system was a damn good system to live under. We discussed the pros and cons for at least an hour more before he felt comfortable with voting guilty. I'm proud of the jury; I think we all feel we made the right decision."*

George had visited briefly with Joseph Palmer following the verdict, agreeing to meet at Palmer's office the following morning at nine o'clock. Palmer greeted George with a warm handshake as he ushered him to a comfortable chair.

"I still can't believe they convicted her," George said. He sat stiff and upright; the dark circles under his eyes, the drawn deep-lined face and the slack of his normally hard-set jaw reflected his restless, fitful sleep just before dawn.

"I knew it would be a close call," Palmer said. "The evidence weighed heavily against her."   George sighed. "What can we do now?"

"As I said last night, we'll appeal regardless of Gina's sentence—that should come in the next few days. In the meantime, we will have to keep Gina's spirits up as best we can."

"Bail?"

"Less likely than before the verdict. Of course, I'll try."

"Do. I'll put up whatever it takes."

"I'll look into it. I have an appointment with the D.A. and Judge Quinn this afternoon."

"If we can get bail or an appeal, then what?"

"Another trial in the appellant court. It would give us time to turn up new evidence—perhaps find the witness in the canyon."

"What is Gina facing in the way of a prison term?"

"Twenty to thirty years. Worst case, life with chance for parole."

"My God! You'll call me as soon as you know something?"

"Yes. It may be late this afternoon."

"I'll be waiting."

The sun had set, the last rays leaving ribbons of brushed gold across the sky. George rested in his favorite chair, looking across the orchard and to the rolling hills beyond. Memories of the early years on the Homeplace dominated his thoughts, temporarily pushing Gina's plight from his mind. He turned to answer the ringing of the telephone.

"George, Joe Palmer. No bail. Quinn feels since he withdrew it in pretrial that it certainly wouldn't be prudent to allow it now that there is a conviction. Sentencing is set for day after tomorrow."

"What's your prognosis on that score?"

"As we discussed earlier, and given the evidence and the verdict, I'm sure Sandburg won't consider a lesser plea, which translates into murder in the first. But we will appeal. We still have alternatives."

"But in the meantime, Gina stays in jail or goes to the State pen?"

"Yes, and I might get relief for bail from the appellant court."
"Odds?"
"Slim to none. They tend to uphold lower court recommendations on bail matters."
"Anything else?"
"One concession from Sandburg. He knows I'm appealing, so he has concurred with my request of Judge Quinn to allow Gina to stay in jail here until the appeal is heard in Spokane."
"That's some conciliation. At least her family will be able to visit her regularly. Thanks, Joe, good-night."

The Homeplace was quiet again, the hush broken only by the soft ticking of the mantle clock. George sat in the darkness, his thoughts now turning to the nightmare of the last few months and Gina's most recent torment. The pledge to keep the family together made to his father so long ago seemed hollow in light of Gina's current situation. Despite his successes in business, he felt a sense of betrayal to his pledge—a sense of failure to his family. *Have I really sacrificed enough?* He would never forgive himself for his father's untimely death. Had he been more attentive at immigration headquarters, the Sternvald name would not have been changed, the visit to the ship would not have been necessary; Father would have lived. His father's death had caused his mother to become withdrawn and finally insane. Her love for him and Anna had withered and died. Brave Anna; without a mother's love, confessing to George her fear of joining her mother in depression and early death. Thank God for her finding love and happiness with Steven Northshield.

Now, what would happen to Gina and her family? Flynn's death, perhaps, in part, as a result of George's rejections—at least his failure to support him in time of crisis? His 'family' at the bank torn and weakened by ugly rumors of a takeover and before that an ambitious man who lacked an ounce of integrity.

Sarah, his devoted, loving, never-demanding Sarah. He had taken her too much for granted—took of her time, gave so little of his in return. She loved him so, and he her. He wondered if she ever knew how much.

Beth—was he moving too quickly? Was Gina right in her judgement of her? He thought not. Beth had been the only positive thing in his life these last months. Now, the final blow. Gina, Margaret, her two fine sons, chastised and held to ridicule by the community—prison for Gina.

My pledge. My word. My failure! George wanted to scream away his agony and pain! To tell the world he was a sham. He bowed his head and cried, body shaking and contorted, as he sought in vain to rid himself of his malady.

Chapter 46

Gina's appeal had been scheduled for a fall hearing so she would remain in the county jail. Beth had been at George's side, listening, comforting, waiting. Their social life had been drastically curtailed during the trial and immediately after, but now was back on a daily basis.

"I need to get away. Let's drive to the cabin and spend the day," George suggested, Beth readily agreeing. After stopping to buy a few essential groceries, they arrived at the cabin shortly before noon. The cabin, more a lodge, enjoyed electrical service but no telephone. It had a large kitchen, living room with rock fireplace, two large bedrooms on the main floor, two more upstairs plus a sleeping loft, and was situated high on a mountainside overlooking Glacier Lake. Outside a stream tumbled by on its way to empty into Swiftwater River.

Access was over a limited use county road that crossed and recrossed the stream on narrow, one- way log bridges built in the 1930s under one of many make-work projects of the Roosevelt era. The one concession to roughing it was the outdoor toilet facilities situated up a small pathway from the back porch. The nearest neighbor some five miles away, the nearest telephone nearly ten. "A truly 'get-away-from-it-all' location, I love it!" George said, pulling his station wagon under the protection of the carport. "Looks like a storm may be brewing. Let's get inside and start a fire, then have lunch."

Thunderclaps ricocheted from the tree-choked mountainsides, sounding as giant tenpins in Mother Nature's bowling alley. Lightning raced across the sky, ripping jagged holes in the boiling, black clouds.

The wind paused, still as death, then roared to life, hurling the torrential downpour onto the landscape, slamming against the log exterior and shake roof of the lodge, sounding like loose gravel pounding the window panes. Within the hour, the rippling stream outside the door was roaring in its channel, hurling small boulders and logs down the valley gorge. A mile away, two bridges were awash, then gone in an instant as the pilings and approach aprons disappeared under tons of water and debris. Inside the lodge the electricity winked out, plunging the interior to near darkness, so dense were the clouds and rain outside. Rain found its way down the chimney, sputtering into tiny puffs of steam as it hit the burning logs; a tree crashed nearby with a heartrending cry, a two hundred-year-old Douglas Fir reduced to a tangle of broken limbs and needles.

"We'll be okay," George assured Beth, who had curled up on the davenport near the fireplace. A chilling dampness permeated the interior, carrying the heavy pungency of wet forestlands. "This will pass in an hour or so, then we'll know what our situation is. Afraid?"

"A little, but as long as you're with me...."

He tucked an afghan around her shoulders, pulling her to him.

As quickly as it came, the storm moved on, the kettledrums of thunder fading over the horizon and the steady drip of water from the roof and surrounding trees giving witness to the storm's passing. The stream flow began to subside, the water running dirty; leaves and pine needles bounced over the rocks, swirling in small eddies before tumbling to the next pool, then on again, toward the valley.

"Nearly five o'clock; be dark soon. Help me with the Coleman lanterns; at least we have light and plenty of dry wood in the box. Cold food for dinner, I'm afraid," George said.

"Who can eat, I'm still trying to recover from the excitement." Beth pulled the comforter around her and moved closer to the fire. George came and stood nearby, hands outstretched to the flames. By nine o'clock news bulletins from the portable radio were reporting the bridge and roadway washouts. George Stern's believed whereabouts were noted and plans made to attempt rescue the next day. The possibility a female companion being with him escaped mention.

"I'm hurt," she pouted girlishly, "I'm here too, you know!" she shouted at the radio, then laughed her low, sultry laugh that sent tingles up George's spine.

Later that evening, following a dinner of meat sandwiches and wine, George said, "We'd better think about sleeping arrangements." He began banking the fire for morning.

The storm had provided the perfect setting, and Beth intended to take full advantage. Moonlight filtered onto the carpet; flame shadows played hide and seek in the dark corners and on the walls and ceiling.

"Darling."

"Yes?" George turned from locking the door.

Beth stood naked before the fire, her body outlined by the embers' red glow. She turned sideways, bending slightly backward, her breasts taut and proud, her auburn hair, aflame with color, cascaded loose and free around her shoulders. "Come here." Her voice low, demanding. "Take off your clothes, my dearest, I want you."

He did her bidding, then moved to her, taking her hot, yielding body to his. She marveled at his physique, still lean and broad-shouldered. The muscles in his arms and legs were strong and smooth. Only the matting of thick white hair across his chest attested to his age. His jaw and neck showed little slackness of one over fifty. She moved against the hardness of his member, felt the light sweat on his arms, heard him whisper her name against her cheek. Lifting her with ease, he walked rapidly to a back bedroom, the soft glow of a candle lighting the room. Beth had been with many men for many reasons, but she intended this performance to be her finest hour. The proper moves, the hands and fingers placed so, the moans and gasps, the whispered endearments, the last thrusts as if orgasm had been achieved—the practiced art of a woman of the night.

He kissed her deeply, his tongue forcing into her mouth; she eagerly responding. His hands gently caressing, lips and tongue setting spot fires on her face, her shoulders, her nipples, her stomach, and lower still until her legs parted and his tongue moved within her. *Control yourself,* she thought, *don't enjoy this too much....* An involuntary moan of delight escaped her lips as she felt moisture. *Oh God, it's not supposed to be this way!* She struggled to regain control, partially succeeding but failing a moment later as he entered her, hard and demanding, thrusting inside her, faster and faster, bodies now moving as one. *No!...No! I'm in charge!* Then, for the first time in her life, a flood of indescribable joy coursed through her body, over and over, growing more fantastic, reaching higher and higher plateaus of pleasure. Her cry, a scream of animal lust filled the room as she felt him burst inside her, his body straining, then gradually less tense until, fully relaxed, he rolled to his side, whispering her name.

My God, what has this man done! Could it be I truly love him? Can it be I can love? The possibility astounded her and made her afraid. *Without control who knows what I might do or allow to happen!* She looked at this kind and wonderful man lying beside her and knew she was in love for the first time in her life. A sudden surge of guilt chilled her and she shook, then began to sob uncontrollably.

"Beth! What is it! Did I hurt you? Tell me what's wrong!" He pulled her close, stroking her hair, kissing away the salty tears. She lay against him, her body goosebumped and cold beneath the warm blankets he'd placed across them.

"I can't tell you now, my dearest...someday, maybe, not now. Oh, George, I love you so very much. *Did I say 'love?' Did I mean it? My God, I did!* Her heart sang for the happiness of the moment. Dark memories tried to crowd in but she pushed them back. *No regrets tonight.* She stopped crying, then used a tissue to dry her eyes. She took his hand and nestled into the curl of his arm and against the pillow. She slept.

. The days that followed, a rescue achieved the next afternoon, were some of the happiest days of their lives for both Beth and George in recent memory. They made love, chatted like two magpies, held hands in public and generally made fools of themselves when no one was watching.

Chapter 47

The announcement of a mid-July wedding between George Stern and a woman nearly twenty years his junior brought raised eyebrows, behind-the-hand whispers, and the major topic on party lines and party talks throughout Aurora. No one doubted Beth's beauty and charm; some questioned her motivation and sincerity. To the two persons affected most, George and Beth, the gossip and innuendos meant little. George had no doubts. Even Gina's persistent harping he pushed aside while wishing she could be more understanding. The two were yet to meet, despite Beth's repeated offers to visit her with George, or alone.

For Beth, a struggle of profound proportion raged within her mind and heart. The fear of what would happen to their relationship should George discover her original motivations in wanting to meet him— or worse yet, her sordid past. Worse yet, her darkest secret of all. She pushed it into her mind's deepest recesses like a childhood nightmare long forgotten. *If I tell myself it didn't happen, maybe it will go away. A secret I will carry to my grave.*

Steve and Anna Northshield arrived two days before the scheduled Saturday nuptials. Small receptions had been held by a few of George's closest business associates. A Friday-evening affair with open invitation at the country club provided opportunity for Stern Enterprise management and staff to attend, close friends and neighbors, the bold and the curious. During the evening, several hundred mingled on the terrace and grounds or inside the clubhouse where food and drink was in abundant supply. A small contingency of guards was on hand in case of trouble. Fortunately, the crowds were well-behaved, and the evening finished without incident.

Doubts any had that love had bloomed for George or Beth was quickly dispelled by the fond and loving exchange of looks and words. As the last guest departed near midnight, Anna took Beth aside into a small anteroom near the entrance. "I so wanted to get to visit with you and get to know you since our brief hellos last night, but the opportunities kept slipping away. Do you mind if we visit a bit now before leaving?"

"No, I'd be delighted."

They sat across from each other. Anna poured a small glass of wine for each, then raised hers in a toast. "May the flowers always return on the tide," Anna said. "An old Hawaiian toast." They smiled and drank.

"I'm so happy you could come! George talks of you so often and how much you've meant to him all these years."

"Yes. I wouldn't miss tomorrow for the world."

They chatted a few minutes before George pushed open the door. "Here you two are; everything okay?"

"Just girl talk, big brother. You and Beth run along; Steve and I will be along shortly."

Chapter 48

Only a handful of closest friends were invited to the wedding; no reception was planned. By one-thirty the guests arrived and were ushered to the north side yard at the Homeplace. An altar was festooned with flowers, as were both sides of the short center aisle. Chairs for the guests sat in even rows along the carpeted center walkway.

In a back bedroom, Beth checked and rechecked her hair and makeup. Dressed in a pale blue sheath dress with matching shoes, a small pillbox hat with attached veil covering the upper portion of her face, and elbow-length velvet gloves, she was a beautiful bride to behold. Her stomach churned with excitement and joy. The minutes could not pass quickly enough.

"May I come in?" Anna asked, pushing open the door.

"Yes, hello." Beth looked past Anna to the two uniformed officers standing behind Anna. "What are they doing here?" she asked, wide-eyed. She felt for and found the bed and sat down, her mouth suddenly dry, her fingers locking and interlocking uncontrollably.

"This is Sheriff Earl Collier and his deputy, Tom Fellows. Both are old friends of my brother."

"I see."

"Miss Ashbrook, pardon me, Miss Young, I'm here to arrest you for the murder of Theodore Jaffey. Here is the warrant." He pushed it forward but she ignored the form. "I must ask you to come with me."

"But how..." She stopped, realizing to say more could hurt any defense she might have. *Damn! Damn! Damn!* She broke into uncontrollable sobs.

"I must tell George and the guests. Would you be so kind as to keep Beth here until everyone has left?" Anna requested.

"Yes'm, be glad to."

Outside the door Anna began to cry softly, motioning Steve to her side. "I'll go up and tell George. Be a dear and ask the wedding party and guests to leave...just tell them there's been a sudden change of plans. Oh, this will kill George, but I had no choice."

Steve hugged her, then kissed her lightly on the mouth before going outside. Anna climbed the stairs, each step flooding back memories of the house she had loved. She tapped lightly on George's door and entered.

Chapter 49

George sat stone-faced, staring bleakly ahead, hardly listening to Sheriff Collier explain the events of the past sixteen hours. Anna sat beside George, holding his limp hand in hers. Steve and Prosecutor Sandburg sat quietly listening.

"When Missus Northshield first came to me with her news...well, I just couldn't believe it. I also realized we had little time to confirm her story. I called the Honolulu police and wired the Young woman's fingerprints lifted from the wineglass Missus Northshield brought us. They confirmed who she was and that she has a long record of arrests from solicitation to running an escort service. She's known as 'Madame Lei' in the Islands. She has also been arrested for gambling and suspected drug sales, but many of those were dismissed for lack of evidence."

Anna picked up the story. "I knew I'd seen her before, but it wasn't until last night at the reception I remembered where. She had been with Barnes at the Honolulu Airport the day he met Ted Jaffey. That was the day before her brother and three others were found murdered in a house near Diamond Head."

Sheriff Collier added to the information. "According to her confession, Ms Young put two and two together and knew Jaffey must have killed her brother. With her brother's murder, she was without income or support. She came to Aurora to blackmail Jaffey but he'd have none of it. She then decided to rob him and got him to open the wall safe. Inside, she found copies of some gambling debts Jaffey owed her brother and her suspicions were confirmed. Jaffey tried to jump her and she shot him, then messed up the place to make it look like a robbery."

"Without her telling you all this, you didn't have a very strong case. Why did she confess?" Sandburg commented.

"I was getting to that next. I got a warrant from Judge Quinn to search her room and deposit box at the Aurora Arms. The .38 was in the box, big as life. We had the murder weapon. With Jaffey gone, she apparently decided to kill two birds with one stone and get revenge on others at the bank. What better way but get Mister Stern in a compromising position. As it turned out, her plan worked better than she'd hoped. Why take a slice of bread when you can have the whole loaf, so to speak. Sorry, Mister Stern, but that's pretty much how her story went down."

"She loves me. I don't care what she says or how it sounds, I know she loves me," George said quietly, almost without emotion. Anna squeezed his hand but said nothing.

"One more thing," Earl said, "there's another real twist to this whole story. Near as I can figure, she was afraid to contact the authorities on the Islands with what she suspected. She apparently thought her past record would be used against her or they'd think she had something to do with killing her brother and the others. Anyway, as Young's sister, she is his sole heir. She's going to inherit an estate worth several million dollars!"

Chapter 50

Gina was released from jail late Saturday evening to the custody of Joe Palmer pending final arraignment of Beth Young before Judge Quinn. For the first time in months Gina was to be with her family, sleep in her own bed. Her ordeal was finally over.

George tried to contact Beth but without success. She refusing his visits to the county jail, his letters were returned unopened. She waived trial and was sentenced at a closed session in Judge's chambers. Within the week, she was transferred to the State prison to begin her life sentence.

As with the death of Sarah, Anna again became George's companion in grief. He held no animosity for her actions, knowing they stemmed from her unconditional love for him. She sheltered him from efforts of the press to gain interviews and pictures; she screened telephone calls, responded to personal letters, shopped and kept house for him. Most importantly, she listened and comforted, watched as his resilient spirit was reborn.

Gina's visit with her father was bittersweet. Without words they held each other, crying, unashamed for each other's joy and sorrow, the bitterness melting away with their tears. "We are family again," said George.

"Never a family like before, never with Flynn not here." Gina's lower jaw trembled. "It's a terrible thing to say, but I'm glad Jaffey is dead!"

"I know you're still full of bitterness, but you must push it aside. By the way, did Anna ask you about a letter and some clippings she mailed you?"

"Yes, I don't remember the letter, why?"

"We put together the dates of Jaffey's sudden request for a vacation, the day Anna saw him at the airport, Young's murder, Anna's best recollection of the date she mailed the letter and clippings, with Flynn's death. Anna suggested, and we agree that it's logical, that her letter may have arrived the day you were in Seattle—remember I tried to contact you?" Gina nodded. George continued, "Suppose Flynn opened the letter, realized what Jaffey must have done, and called him over to the house. They argue, somehow Jaffey subdues Flynn and makes it look like a suicide, destroys the evidence and is basically home free. At the time of Flynn's 'suicide,' Anna and Steve had just left for an extended business trip. They didn't get back until after your trial. She had no reason to think her letter went undelivered and may have caused Flynn's death. If anything, she might have thought the letter contributed to your conviction as evidence. For whatever reasons, the letter didn't come up until a few days ago."

"What you're saying is we can never prove Jaffey killed Flynn," Gina said bitterly. "You're right; some will always believe Flynn was a crook and that he committed suicide.

Even if we had Jaffey's written confession in our hands, there'd still be doubters. That's human nature."

"Sage words, Daddy, but it still doesn't take away my loneliness and hate of what happened."

Chapter 51

The ordeal was over. George Stern rested, the Homeplace weaving its healing spell. The heartaches he had wrestled with so recently were still within him, but not as strong and hurtful. His love and faith in Gina, again fulfilled, brought peace of mind. He walked to the side porch and stood, listening to the sounds of an autumn afternoon. It was quiet now, the rush of harvest over, a season for beauty and reflection. He no longer railed against the coming winter, for he was now at peace.

* * *